PERIL AT PIG'S-EYE CAVE

Peril at Pig's-Eye Cave

A Doc and Tweed History Mystery

John Koblas

NORTH STAR PRESS OF ST. CLOUD, INC.

ISBN: 0-87839-209-2

Art by: Billy Laakkonen and Chase Clausing
Cover Art: Billy Laakkonen

First Edition

Printed in the United States of America by
Versa Press, East Peoria, Illinois

Published by
North Star Press of St. Cloud, Inc.
P.O. Box 451
St. Cloud, Minnesota 56302
nspress@cloudnet.com

contents

what is a history mystery?

The purpose of this Doc and Tweed adventure is twofold. First, and most obvious, it's to be read for the mystery, for the adventure. Second, and just as important, students learn to identify people, places, events, and objects important in Minnesota as well as United States history. By keeping the action fast-paced and the answer to the riddle just beyond one's fingertips, readers find themselves learning history without really being aware of it. History really is fun and never boring if presented correctly. Each Doc and Tweed story is designed to both please and educate readers and to enable them to use problem-solving and critical-thinking skills, analyze clues, and explore topics and events from the past.

WARNING!!!

Doc and Tweed beg you: Stay out of caves. In addition to frequent cave-ins, there are many other dangers which may result in serious injury or death. Caves often contain elevated levels of carbon dioxide; consequently you may be putting yourself at risk without really knowing the danger. This invisible danger is only one of many hazards to be encountered in caves. Never go into a cave without adult supervision.

Chapter One

afloat

"Looks like it's going to be another great summer," George "Doc" Diezel said between yawns, as the small motorboat skimmed the waters of St. Paul's Crosby Lake. George, frequently called Doc, was meticulous about nearly everything he did. He also had a penchant for reading Doc Savage novels from the 1930s and 1940s. A bit unusual for a fourteen-year old, but Doc Diezel was a reader, something his teachers always said as if in capital letters—"Doc, the READER."

"Don't lean so close to the water or you won't be here for another summer," his lanky friend Tweed Salter said, taking a piece of licorice candy from his mouth to give the warning, then pushing the soggy rope back in again.

Doc merely smiled, rolled over on his back, and saluted the morning sky. Tweed Salter was Doc's best friend, but Doc didn't know everything about the boy. Where the name Tweed had come from, for example. This, of course, wasn't his friend's real name—it was short for something or other—but Doc knew enough about Tweed to appreciate that, he didn't want his block knocked off, he wouldn't ask him about his name. Maybe it stood for Tweety or Twickenham or something embarrassing. As far as Doc was concerned, if his friend liked to be called Tweed, Tweed he was.

Doc loved spending time in St. Paul with his older sister, Elizabeth Decker, and her husband, Andy. Nearly every summer, his parents would let him go to St. Paul for at least few days to a week. This year he'd be there nearly until school started again, two whole weeks away. He liked the Twin Cities so much better than Wood Dale, Illinois, where he lived, and he was fond of his older sister and her husband. Mostly, though, and he couldn't wait to see his best friend, Tweed, whom he had met during one of his first visits in St. Paul some five years before.

Two solid weeks of living Huck Finn style—Doc dreamed of this all year long. He firmly believed that there was no better

woodsman or tour guide in the world than fourteen-year-old Tweed Salter. But while Doc often fantasized about days spent with Tweed, he couldn't really envy him. The boy's life had not been easy. Both of Tweed's parents had been killed in a car accident before he had learned to walk. Since then he had lived with his grandfather, Joe West, in a cabin well back in the woods from Mendota. Joe might live near the hustle and bustle of St. Paul, Minnesota's capital city, but he didn't hold too highly with "new-fangled civilization" as he liked to refer to it. Tweed had never enjoyed television at Joe's house, nor microwaves or dishwashers. Joe still heated with wood he cut and split himself, and lighted the little cabin with kerosene lanterns.

Tweed Salter had never attended any of the schools in Mendota Heights or the larger facility in Inver Grove Heights. He said he had special permission from the school board to be tutored by his grandfather—home schooled he called it. Doc knew Tweed's grandfather had to be plenty smart because no one knew more about history, reading, science, or math than Tweed. Tweed's grandfather would always say, "Books and learning are very important things. Hunting, fishing, and navigating the river are too." Thus Tweed knew as much about the natural world as any Boy Scout and more about history than anyone Doc knew. Doc suspected that if Mrs. Malory, his history teacher all of eighth grade, would have called him a READER too.

"Where shall we take the boat today?" Tweed said with an edge to the words as if he had already asked the question more than once.

Doc blinked at him.

Tweed rolled his eyes. "You're not paying attention. Where do you want to go? We can take the Mississippi east to St. Paul or head up the river to Pike Island where Zebulon Pike raised the American flag for the first time in Minnesota in 1805."

Doc looked up the river. He liked almost anything they thought of to do, and Pike Island seemed interesting enough, but he didn't want to settle for the first choice. Tweed might come up with something more interesting.

Almost to himself, Tweed continued. "Pike bought nine miles on each side of the river from the Sioux, and they put the first military post in Minnesota fifteen years later."

"Sounds interesting enough," Doc said, tentatively.

"And there above you, Doc," said Tweed, pointing, "see the Round Tower at Fort Snelling—that was built in 1820, the very first building erected in Minnesota by Americans—other, of course, than Native Americans."

Doc looked up as the tower slipped past them. "This Zebulon Pike . . . is he the same guy they named Pike's Peak in Colorado after?"

"Yup, one and the same," said Tweed, flashing Doc a smile that seemed to congratulate him on his history knowledge. He steered the little boat around a dead head of an old stump, then pointed again. "Hey, and across the river we could stop at the Henry H. Sibley House—the oldest surviving home in the state."

"Really? Is it interesting?"

"Sure. It was built in 1835 of limestone blocks cemented with mud from the riverbanks. The inside walls and ceilings were made of grasses and willow branches woven together, then plastered with mud by Sioux women. Oh, and next door is the Jean Baptiste Faribault House. It was built only four or five years later. Faribault was a pioneer, a fur trader, and a friend of both local natives and missionaries."

Doc looked where Tweed pointed. He could tell his friend was on a roll, but looking at houses didn't sound perfect enough for the day. Something really good for them to explore would come to Tweed soon.

"Just up the hill is the 1854 Hypolite De Puis House, the home of Sibley's private secretary, and St. Peter's Catholic Church, the oldest church in continuous use in the state. That was built in 1853 from limestone quarried nearby."

Tweed seemed to be reaching. Doc wasn't sure what to hope for next. Then Tweed turned to Doc and grinned. "Or, we could just take it kind of easy. I know a creek in the heart of the river bottoms that is as much fun as the Everglades."

Doc grinned. This was better than houses.

Just then, Tweed's dog, Mustard, jumped into the water and went paddling after a family of ducks that had stopped to look the boys over. There were seldom any other boats on Crosby Lake since the lake was somewhat of a backwater. With all the popular swimming lakes in Minneapolis and St. Paul, few people paid any attention at all to the wild marshland of Crosby, that is, if they knew of it at all. Just the kind of place for Joe West to know and show his grandson.

"Ho, Mustard," Tweed shouted after his dog, a mixture between a terrier and a beagle and who knew what else. The little twenty-pound dog was putting some distance between himself and the boat, stroking hard after the ducks. Mustard, mostly white with big yellow spot across his back, had one ear that kind of stood up, and the other flopped. He had a few wiry whiskers on his face and a tail that had been cropped to a short little stub. Joe West had found him, skinny and homeless, two years before, and he had been Tweed's constant companion ever since.

"Come back, boy. C'mon back," Tweed called as the ducks decided to head out into the main part of the lake and the little dog gamely offered to follow.

Of all the dogs Doc Diezel had ever known, although he had to admit he was not on intimate terms with too many, Mustard was the most obedient animal he had ever seen. As much as Mustard wanted those ducks, he turned around and began paddling back to the boat. Tweed pulled him back aboard, and just like most wet dogs—and his short yellow and white coat could hold a surprising lot of water—Mustard shook himself, drenching both boys.

"Doggone it," Tweed said, wiping his face, "I sure didn't want a bath this early in the morning."

"Oh, well," Doc laughed, wiping the lake water from his chin and picking a few bits of duck weed off his jeans, "I'll bet Zebulon Pike endured hardships a lot worse than this when he was fourteen like us."

"Okay, okay," Tweed said, and grinned. "So, are you going to tell me where you want to go before the sun goes down? We aren't wearing these life jackets just for looks. Let's get some use out of them. There's history, legends, and excitement in every direction from here. Ah-ha! I've got an idea."

Doc wasn't so sure. Tweed sure seemed on a building kick that morning, and Doc wanted more adventure than architecture. "Aw, now listen. I don't want to walk around some old house or church." He realized how comfortable he was in the bottom of the boat, so he added, "If your idea means any paddling, climbing, or anything remotely associated with work, I want nothing to do with that either. I just want to lay on the river, take in some of that good old sun, and forget that school will be starting again in another two weeks."

Doc saw something flash across Tweed's face, an unhappy, almost jealous, kind of look. Doc wondered if he really wanted to go to public school. But the look passed almost instantly, and Tweed said, "We could go upstream a little ways to old Fort Snelling, look the fort over and pretend we're soldiers stationed on the prairie."

Doc wrinkled his nose. "Naw! We did that last summer. If you remember, that old guy escorted us off the premises for scaring the daylights out of him."

"He was just a crazy old coot."

Doc lifted his head and raised his eyebrows. He would have raised one dramatically, but they didn't work separately. "You dressed up like Colonel Snelling and told the old guy the fort was under attack. He thought you were some kind of ghost."

Tweed gave his companion a disgusted roll of the eyes and shut off the motor. "Okay, let's stay right here on Crosby Lake then," he suggested. There's history here too, you know. There used to be an old farm on the eastern end of the lake. There are miles and miles of hiking trails here, including a bog trail between two lakes. I've seen deer here, and woodchucks, raccoons, rabbits, squirrels, and all kinds of birds. The most amazing thing is we are in the middle of a total wilderness within only a few miles of downtown St. Paul."

"That's kinda cool," Doc agreed.

"I can show you some strange open swamp areas, deeper woods than we saw in that preserve in Wood Dale a couple years ago, and some Renoir fields of yellow, blue, and purple wildflowers."

Doc Diezel was not impressed with looking at wildflowers. After all, he had come to Minnesota looking for adventure. What did buildings and wildflowers have to do with that? And though puttering through a swamp had its merits, they'd probably end up swatting hordes of mosquitoes for the effort.

Tweed, however, had his own agenda. He wanted to do *something*. He wanted Doc to agree to one of the plans he had thought of or offer something else. When Doc didn't do that, he started to get frustrated. "Okay, then, let's go down below the fort where the Mississippi and Minnesota rivers meet," he suggested. "Right there is Pike Island, and that's a lot of island waiting to be explored. Maybe we can hunt for buried treasure or something. I found a lot of arrowheads there last fall, and once I even found an old jar with some funny writing on it."

7

"Are there any caves down there?" Doc inquired, beginning to show a little interest.

"Caves! If you want to see caves, we've got two of the biggest around. Have you ever heard of Carver Cave or Fountain Cave?

Doc sat up. Neither name seemed to ring a bell in his consciousness. He thought he had read about the explorer Jonathan Carver somewhere—perhaps in one of his history books.

"Carver Cave is a lot bigger," said Tweed, "but Fountain Cave is a lot closer, especially when I'm the one who has to maneuver this boat down river."

Doc grinned. Now this sounded like the kind of adventure he'd hoped to have with Tweed. "Caves," he said. "Yup, that's just the ticket."

Tweed grinned back. "Great. If you're ready, we'll head out onto the river. Make sure that life jacket is on tight."

Of course, the boys had no intention of entering the cave should they actually find the opening. They'd have plenty of fun just searching for the entrance since it had been covered up by the extension of Shepard Road in the 1960s. Tweed didn't mention that they had not packed sandwiches or made up a thermos of Kool-Aid to tide them over to supper. Doc had seemed listless enough without making him lose all his enthusiasm for the expedition.

With Doc sitting up straight for the first time that morning, the boys had little trouble finding their way out of the marsh and onto the strong current of the Mississippi. As the sun soared toward its zenith, the boys followed the St. Paul bank of the river. Once Doc thought he heard a bullfrog croaking from somewhere on the bank, but he saw nothing. With the sound of the motor roaring in his ears, he couldn't be sure of anything. Still, the croaking sound seemed real, and he shuddered a bit when he realized the groaning seemed to say, "Don't go! Don't go!" Of course, he didn't say anything about this to Tweed.

The taller, more muscular Minnesota boy kept his eyes on the river, and he was all business. Joe West had taught him well. Normally, two fourteen-year olds would not be on the river alone, but Tweed had grown up on the river, and there was not a turn or an eddy that he didn't know. Joe trusted them.

"Mom said we better not get into trouble this summer," Doc offered quietly as the boat slid into the current and speeded up.

Tweed slanted his eyes in his friend's direction, "You mean not like last summer or the summer before that?"

"Or the one before that," said Doc. "and, oh, the first summer, too. Yeah, she said we're getting older and should learn to keep out of trouble."

"What's the fun in that?"

Doc remembered the time they tried to catch that ghost at Fort Snelling or when they tried to save a pretty girl from going over St. Anthony Falls in a barrel. Trouble wasn't something on back alleys or hidden in dumpsters for him and Tweed; trouble seemed to be one of their pals tagging at their heels. It had a dizzying habit of finding them whether they had good intentions or not. "What the heck," said Doc. "We'll worry about that later when we think of something with trouble attached to it. All we're doing is *looking* for a cave. There's not a lick of any trouble in that. Right?"

"Right," said Tweed. "We don't get anywhere near trouble unless we actually *find* the cave and think about going in it. *That* could be trouble. People have *died* in those caves."

Doc watched a red-winged blackbird swoop down near the shore and disappear into a thicket. At almost the same moment, a large carp jumped out of the water and re-entered the murky depths in the flicker of an eye, or, more specifically, the swish of its tail. It was almost as if these local residents were all saying, "Good-bye, have a nice trip!"

The little motor worked steadily, and the boat passed swiftly down the river, but Tweed knew how to keep it under control. His hand never left the tiller. Doc could not help but think about how helpless he would be on the river if anything ever happened to Tweed. He gave a moment's thought to the idea that trouble could easily find them on the Mississippi River—get the boat in trouble with barges or bigger boats—but he trusted his friend's river skills. Anyway, maybe trouble would go bother someone else this summer and leave him and Tweed to their fun. He didn't give much thought to the fact that looking for caves actually had been his own idea, not Tweed's. But the idea that the Mississippi River, which emerged from Lake Itasca in northern Minnesota, cut down through the entire nation on its way to the Gulf of Mexico did occur to him. Mississippi was a big river, an important river. He knew he'd have lots to tell his friends back in Wood Dale. He usually did at the end of each visit. At the moment, however, his mind had fixed on Fountain Cave, wondering most if they could find it. He could almost picture the place. How beautiful the name sounded, creating images of soft cascades of water and a ferny entrance.

"Fountain Cave is pretty, right?" he asked Tweed.

Tweed shrugged. "'Round here, most people called Fountain Cave Pig's-Eye."

"Pig's-Eye?" Doc stammered, his daydream of great cascades of water covering the entrance to the cave drying up. Pig's-Eye didn't give him nearly as pleasant an image. "Where on earth did it get a crazy name like that?"

"Pig's-Eye Cave is named after Pierre 'Pig's-Eye' Parrant. He was one of the early settlers in this region . . . not-too-honest a one either, I guess. He used Fountain Cave for smuggling. He'd sell all kinds of stuff to the Indians and the soldiers from Fort Snelling right out of the cave. My grandfather said that at night there'd be strange goings-on in Pig's-Eye Cave, and some very weird people would be seen leaving."

"Okay, but why did they call *him* Pig's-Eye?" asked Doc. Smuggling and weird people had his enthusiasm growing.

"His real name was Pierre Parrant. He was a French-Canadian. He wore a patch over one eye that he was kinda blind in. I suppose since he couldn't see out of that eye anyway, and because of that awful patch and his shady dealings, they called him Pig's-Eye."

"Maybe we'll find some of Pig's-Eye's loot in that cave."

Tweed made a face. "We not going to find anything in the cave. Not Pig's-Eye's loot or anything else. We're just going to *look* for the cave. If we find it, we're *not* going in. Caves are dangerous. That would get us in the most trouble yet. Anyway, Slim—that tall kid you met last summer—and I explored that cave pretty good with a spelunker's club led by a professional cave guide from the university. That was a couple years ago, and we didn't find a thing of any use then."

"Yeah, but you could have missed something. Maybe there's a small passageway leading to a hidden chamber. Wouldn't it be neat if Parrant had a glass-eye, and it was still in that cave? What if we found *that*?"

Tweed Salter did not answer. He slipped another stick of licorice into his mouth and jerked the boat to the left to keep it on course. By hugging the bank, he could maneuver the boat to suit his purpose. If there were any shallow sandbars, and, of course, there were few on such a river, he could control the boat with one of the oars.

A dog barked from the shore, and the boys had quite a chore keeping Mustard from jumping into the river again. If ever there was a dog that could get into mischief, it was Mustard. It was the terrier in him, Joe West often told them. Of course, the real reason was probably because he belonged to Tweed, and that capital "T" stood not only for Tweed but also for trouble. Once the bigger dog was out of sight, Tweed let Mustard go, and as if nothing had happened, the dog curled up at his feet and went quickly to sleep.

Occasionally boats—usually far bigger ones—would pass them, but their passengers seldom saw the boys in the shadows of the shoreline. When someone aboard one of the boats did see them, they would usually wave, shout or sound their horn. The boys waved back out of a sense of respect for others—that was part of the fun on the river—but their minds were focused now. Not too far ahead of them lay Pig's-Eye Cave, a real smugglers' den, and maybe there was even the ghost of a pirate.

Where the river separated St. Paul from Lilydale, Tweed brought the boat ashore and told Doc to watch it for a few minutes. Then he and Mustard disappeared over a weedy hill and were gone for about twenty minutes. When they returned, Tweed had an arm-full of apples that he had picked in a wild orchard. The boys sat down to a lunch of sour apples, and Doc roared when he discovered that Mustard ate them too. Back on the river, their hunger eased, they returned to their steady course toward Fountain Cave.

As the eager explorers approached the foot of Otto Avenue, Tweed tugged on his partner's arm and exclaimed, "Right over there someplace is Fountain Cave. Of course, it'll be hard to find. It's been covered with junk, and the highway construction filled in most of the ravine. But I think it'll be easier to find the entrance from the water than looking down from above."

"Tweed, look," the smaller boy exclaimed, pointing to the shore beneath a steep bank. "There's a little boat there, and it doesn't look like anyone's in it."

Tweed killed the motor and used the oars to ease the boat toward shore. "Keep your voice down," he said. "This is kind of strange. No one knows how to get in the cave, but that boat isn't anchored there for nothing. We'll pull up to shore here and make our way on foot the rest of the way. It might be someone curious about the area or . . . it could be something more."

The two boys and the dog clambered from their boat, made sure it rested fully on the bank so the current couldn't pull it back into the water and proceeded through the brambles in the direction of the cave. Wild raspberries, blackberries, and nettles made the going painful, and, since their season had passed, they didn't even offer a sweet morsel in return. Several times, rocks and sand shifted below their feet, and they skidded downward a few feet. At one point, Doc nearly tumbled into the river when he caught his foot on a tangle of Virginia creeper and wild grape vines.

Mustard led the way, but, small as he was, he was somewhat oblivious to thorns and sharp branches. Maybe he even followed rabbit trails under the worst of the thorns.

"Ouch!"

Tweed looked back at Doc. "You okay?"

"I've got scratches all over me," Doc said, showing Tweed his arms that were already crisscrossed with red lines. His white socks were flecked with blood from his shins, which were even worse. "Are you sure it wouldn't be easier to climb up to Shepard Road and make our way back down nearer the cave?"

Tweed crossed his lips with his index finger. "Not if we don't want to be seen. I want to know why that boat is there with nobody around. By the bristles on the back of my neck, I just have a funny feeling about this."

Doc couldn't tell if Tweed was in adventure mode or really worried about how the boat got there. It didn't matter. Goose bumps mixed with the scratches on his arms.

13

A loud boom came from somewhere in front of them. Both boys hit the dirt.

"He's shooting at us!" Doc said in a harsh whisper. "Keep your head down. Mustard! Mustard, get back here!"

The little dog had not barked at the boom and disappeared ahead of them. Tweed stood up slowly and wiped the dirt from his clothing and brushed pebbles and sand from his knees. He looked back at Doc and offered a lop-sided grin. "That wasn't a shot. It scared me too," he said, "but it wasn't a shot. No one's shooting at us."

"How can you be sure?" said Doc, his eyes wide, not as ready to stand up and make a target of himself.

Tweed shook his head. "It wasn't gunfire. That was a barge. They're all over the river, and there's always a lot of clanging and banging. Look across the river. See, they look like great sea turtles. They usually carry grain downstream or coal and chemicals upstream. They bang and bump each other all the time. There . . . see the tugboat over there? What we heard was probably when it connected with that barge it's pushing."

Doc got to his feet slowly, still uncertain. He tried to smile, but he was too embarrassed to say anything.

The pair scampered over large boulders, then hung onto each other as they crossed a ravine choked with wild grapevines, loose rock, and brambles. Over the centuries, the Mississippi River had carved a wide passage for itself, but trying to follow the shore on foot wasn't always easy. Soft mucky places sucked at their shoes, streams cut deep gouges all along the way, and the banks sometime rose steeply. Directly above them they could hear traffic moving along Shepard Road and, farther down river, they saw the Jonathan Paddleford, a packet boat carrying tourists who wanting to view the river bluffs.

Though they had needed nearly half an hour to make their way about a hundred feet along the shore, finally, they reached the site where Fountain Cave was supposed to be. Tweed held his finger to his lips while his other hand grasped Mustard's collar. Slowly they crept out of the thicket and explored the area. Chucks of concrete from the road construction mixed with the rocky ground, giving the landscape a broken, rough appearance. Clumps of raspberry had taken hold, and much of the ground was covered with wild morning glory vines and wild cucumbers, making a thick mat and climbing over everything.

They picked their way carefully, not wanting to trip with so much broken concrete and glass underfoot, but, to their disappointment, they found no one, not even the owner of the boat. They didn't even find the cave entrance. Even though Tweed had visited the cave a few years earlier, since that time it seemed to have been walled up by solid rock.

"But why would somebody just leave a boat here?" Doc asked, somewhat perplexed.

"I don't know," said Tweed. "Maybe it's someone just hiking along the river or eating a picnic lunch somewhere nearby."

"And you're sure this is where the cave was?"

"Pretty sure. Not much of an adventure, was it? What say we head back up river for some of my granddad's flapjacks?"

Doc hesitated, still wondering about the abandoned motorboat. His legs and arms looked like he'd been fighting with angry cats, and stinging nettle burns tingled over his hands and one cheek. If someone only wanted to have a picnic, this wouldn't have been the place to do it unless it was Rambo. Yet someone left that boat tied up to the shore. Doc smelled a mystery, and, if Tweed knew the river and the history of the area, Doc knew mysteries. Still he agreed with his chum that the flapjacks sounded mighty good. The sour apples hadn't held his hunger back much. Perhaps they could return to Fountain Cave the next day to see if the boat was still there.

As they began the hike back to their own motorboat, they both heard a muffled thud behind them. Turning around at a point where a small elm grew almost sideways in an effort to touch the river, the boys saw a somewhat tall, powerfully built man emerging from among the rocks. The stranger looked up and down the river before stepping out of his stone hideaway. He paused there a moment, then turned and disappeared back into the rocks. He had not seen the boys.

Tweed looked at Doc, his mouth open, and Doc looked back, his eyes wide. Then Tweed started back up toward the rocks. His heart thumping in his chest, Doc followed him. They quickly picked their way over the vines and rocks to the spot where they had seen the man. To their amazement, nothing was there but more rocks.

"There *has* to be a secret passage here someplace. That man didn't just plain disappear into thin air," whispered Doc.

Mustard arrived on the scene, panting heavily and covered in bits of stickers and leaves from having followed some rabbit through the weeds.

"Listen!" said Tweed, grabbing Mustard and holding his hand around the dog's mouth. "I hear voices."

Both boys immediately looked down towards the river, but they saw no one. Still the faint undertone of voice clearly came to them, although neither boy could make out what was being said.

"Doc," Tweed whispered, "I think you have your mystery. Those voices are *not* coming from the river." He turned and started back toward the boat.

Doc looked after him. "What do you mean?"

"Don't you get it?" Tweed said, his eyes fixed on the under his feet. "Those voices are coming from *beneath* the ground!"

16

Chapter Two

the st. paul shuffle

The following morning, the two boys rode the bus down West Seventh Street, which Tweed pointed out had once been called the Old Fort Road. They had decided to go to Randolph Avenue and try to walk down to the Fountain Cave site from there. Tweed figured they might be able to see if the motorboat was still tied to the shore or if any suspicious characters lurked about the rock face. After a brief vigil, they planned to get back on the bus and visit the St. Paul Library to look up material on Fountain Cave, Pig's-Eye Parrant, and maybe even Carver Cave. Perhaps they would find something to give them a clue as to what might be going on at Pig's-Eye.

As the city bus eased its way down Seventh Street in morning traffic, both boys were letting their imaginations get away from them.

"What if that boat *is* still there?" Doc asked.

"We'll worry about that when we get there," Tweed answered. "If those galoots are up to something, we may have to bag them."

Doc loved it when Tweed talked like a cop. It fueled his own growing excitement. When the bus arrived at their stop, the two boys all but leapt out and sprinted down Randolph Avenue towards the river. On the way, they crossed several industrial warehouse parking lots and climbed over a barricade or two. Staying on the street wasn't nearly the fun of taking short cuts.

When they reached the small parking area at the Fountain Cave Historical Marker on Shepard Road, they slowed down and tried to watch everything around them. Three cars were parked in the lot in front of the marker. Just as they were arriving, they watched an elderly couple reading the stone plaque. The old couple smiled, greeting them as they turned away. They walked to their car and drove off in the direction of downtown St. Paul.

"That leaves two cars," said Doc, as if that were profound information, "and there's nobody around. Maybe these cars belong to some of our mysterious friends from yesterday."

There is no trail leading down the cliff, and a couple warning signs discouraged unauthorized cave exploring, but the boys moved down the hill slowly and carefully, holding on to branches, twigs, rocks—anything to keep them from falling. It was a steep climb. Part way down the cliff, they noticed that the boat that had been there the day before was gone. But they didn't see anyone who might have driven the cars, either.

Sweating, the boys reached the spot where they had heard voices. They caught their breaths and listened hard for the muffled low tones they had heard. All they could hear was the wind.

"There's no one here now," Doc said, disappointed, but then offered, "Maybe they're so deep in the cave we just can't hear them."

Tweed sighed and started up the cliff face. "Those two cars could belong to sightseers who parked and hopped a bus. Do you think we just imagined those voices yesterday?"

Doc shrugged, looking up at the wicked climb they faced. Going up was always harder.

When the boys reached Seventh Street, drenched in sweat, bug bit and scratched, the bus was just approaching the corner.

"At least we have some good luck working for us," Tweed said.

The boys sprinted for the bus and climbed aboard. Several people looked at them funny, probably wondering at their dirty knees, sweaty faces and the bits of green stuck in their hair. They rode the bus to Kellogg Boulevard and walked up St. Peter, where they purchased hot dogs and root beer from a vendor in Rice Park. They sat down next to the statue of author F. Scott Fitzgerald to devour their lunch. Doc threw bits of bun to the pigeons that gathered for a handout.

In the library, they found a great deal of material on what they were seeking.

"Listen to this," Doc said to his companion. "People knew about the cave as early as 1811. Explorer Stephen H. Long visited it in 1817. Long even said, it was 'far more curious and interesting' than Carver Cave. Hey, Tweed, there's even an underground river in it. Listen: 'To beautify and embellish the scene, a fine crystal stream flows through the cavern and cheers the lonesome dark retreat with its enlivening murmurs.' Maybe those guys in the cave pulled their boat in there and left it on the hidden stream."

Tweed looked up. "That's cool."

Doc was skimming the book in front of him. "And Henry R. Schoolcraft was here in 1820. He discovered the source of the Mississippi River, too. That was later, in 1832. Wow, even the French scientist Joseph R. Nicollet went into the cave in 1837."

"Get this," replied Tweed, sitting across the table from him and scanning his own big book. "There was a big ravine near the cave where Pig's-Eye Parrant set up an illegal business in 1838. The end of that was probably where the raspberries scraped us up the most. His 'Pig's-Eye Pandemonium' was the first building to go up in St. Paul. I knew that. Hey, and this guy who wrote about Parrant said he just mysteriously disappeared one day. Listen to this: 'Very few cared to know why he went, and some were glad that he had really gone.'"

"Maybe he was murdered," said Doc.

Tweed shrugged. "Then this priest, Father Lucien Galtier, built the little log cabin church called the Chapel of St. Paul on the spot in 1841, and most of the settlers who went there built their homes all around Parrant's cave shack. At first, they called the settlement 'Pig's-Eye,' after Parrant, but then Parrant left mysteriously, and the people changed the name of the settlement to St. Paul Landing."

"Certainly a nicer name," Doc said with a chuckle.

Tweed looked at his companion across the table. "If Parrant set up this illegal business there, maybe the guy we saw copied his idea," he said. "It'd still make a great place for smugglers, especially if they had a secret entrance."

The two met gaze lines across the table. Doc said, "We saw that man, and we heard those mysterious voices coming from the ground."

Tweed nodded solemnly. "Those guys got into the cave system somehow. Doc, I really think we might be onto something."

20

The boys pondered these questions as they left the library and headed back to Rice Park. They congratulated themselves on not doing anything that would get them into all the trouble they had found the summers previous. The two amateur detectives sat down on the edge of "The Source," a fountain built after World War II by Alonzo Hauser. Some children ran to the fountain and waded in. Doc and Tweed, victims of an occasional splashing, some of it on purpose, moved away from the fountain and took refuge under some fine tall elms.

As Tweed gazed at the imposing Landmark Center across the street, he fixed his eyes on the turrets, towers, and figures in relief. He saw the relief of a bat. For a moment, the impressive bat dazzled him, but then his eyes noticed something even more intriguing.

"Doc," he whispered, "Don't look now, but do you see those two guys standing on the corner over there? They seem to be watching us. And I'm pretty sure I saw the one in the hat behind us on Fourth Street."

The boys turned down St. Peter Street towards the river, took a left on Kellogg Boulevard, and walked along the bluff through downtown. As they turned on Kellogg, Doc noticed the mysterious pair of men walking in the same direction but staying a good half-block behind them. The art deco county courthouse loomed across the street as the boys passed benches and stately shade trees in a well-landscaped lawn. At Minnesota Street, they glided by the simple stone monument to Father Lucien Galtier. Below them, they gazed at the train tracks that paralleled Shepard Road and the river, and in the distance they saw some oil tanks, the Northern State Power Building with its winking eye, beautiful Harriet Island, and the city's fascinating bridges. They made a great show of taking in all the sights. All the while, however, they kept an eye on the two men, who still followed them.

Looking back over his shoulder, Tweed pretended to be searching for the High Bridge upriver, where in the mid-1800s, young Billy Stiles, who may have been a member of the infamous Jesse James Gang, had jumped into the river. The men still followed them.

Crossing the intersection at Minnesota Street, the boys turned back on Kellogg and began walking back the way they had come. Tweed elbowed his friend as both boys saw only one of their pursuers crossing the street and continuing to stay directly behind them. The other man, the one with the slouch hat, turned also, but followed them from the other side of the street.

"When we get to the corner, let's take a right up Cedar Street," said Tweed in hushed tones. "They're definitely following us. Why, I don't know, but these guys could be dangerous."

"I bet they are the ones who had their cars parked at Fountain Cave," said Doc. "I bet they saw us snooping around and followed the bus in one of their cars. Heck, I bet they saw us go into the library, eat those hot dogs in Rice Park, the whole kaboodle."

Reaching the intersection, the boys turned right and began moving up Cedar.

"Pretend like we don't know they are following us," said Tweed. "Hit me—but light, and kind of shadow box. Maybe they'll think we are just out horsing around and will leave."

The ruse did not work, however. The two mysterious men continued their vigil. At Fifth Street, the boys walked across the Garden Plaza adjoining the Osborn Building and stepped through the collage of greenery and red metal sculpture. Pausing at Alexander Liberman's sculpture, they turned towards Wabasha Street and the Northern Federal Savings and Loan Building with its eerie glass.

"Maybe we better run into one of these buildings," said Doc, starting to feel a little nervous. "Or stop somebody and tell them these men are after us."

"What! And spoil a really good adventure," replied Tweed. "We can lose these guys in a minute any time we want or my name isn't T-W-E, well, Salter. We'll give them the slip at the courthouse. I promise that's as far as we go. If they can't be fooled, we'll just stop a police officer, and that's that!"

The boys began a zigzag route that took them back and forth over several of the same blocks in a three- to four-block square area. Their pursuers seemed to lag a bit—perhaps the boys were wearing out the older men—but still they followed. Pointing to a door at the Ramsey County Courthouse and St. Paul City Hall, Tweed did a fast sidestep with Doc at his heels.

"In here," said Tweed. Once inside, the boys raced to Carl Milles' towering sculpture, "Indian God of Peace," a thirty-six-foot Indian god carved of white Mexican onyx. Looking about the dark-blue marble lobby and seeing no sign of the two men, Tweed pushed Doc behind the giant marble statue.

"Don't breath, don't cough, and *don't* move," ordered Tweed Salter. "I think they just walked in the door and are looking around for us. I am thinking that, since they don't see us walking down the hall, they'll go upstairs. When they do that, we'll give 'em the slip."

Tweed was correct in his assumption. The two men glanced down the long hallway past the tall statue and rushed up the stairs. It required every ounce of courage for Tweed to take a peek at the stairs as he listened to the echo of retreating footsteps.

"Let's go," whispered Doc in heavy half-breaths, as he rose from a crouch. But Tweed had corralled him by the collar, and Doc could not break the powerful grip of his St. Paul friend.

"Not yet! Not Yet!" whispered Tweed. "Stand perfectly still. No, try to get back more behind the statue."

"But . . . but, they're gone. Now's our chance. Maybe our *only* chance!"

"Get down," husked Tweed, as he pushed his friend deeper into the shadows. "Up there . . . Look!"

Doc looked up. Just adjacent to the Indian god's head, he saw the two men staring down from a balcony. They could almost reach out and touch the onyx figure, then shinny down it. As Doc crawled farther toward the back of the statue, his shaking body had to be restrained by the other boy.

"I don't think they saw us, Tweed," he said. "I don't think they did. This is . . . I'm really scared."

The two men just stood there above us—looking, watching, waiting. They were directly above the boys.

"We're trapped like rats if they spot us," Doc said, making himself even smaller in the shadow of the sculpture.

Tweed rolled his eyes. "Not in a public building. We can call out for help at any time, and those guys'll be arrested. If you really want me to, I'll call out right now."

That was too much for Doc. "No!" He unfolded himself a little. "I'm a little scared, yes, but I want to solve this mystery too. If we end the adventure too soon, we'll solve nothing."

Tweed grinned. "Right," he said. Then his face became determined. He peeked up. "I can't see the face of the one wearing that ugly hat but that other one seems to have a nasty scar on the side of his mouth. Some palooka must have got hold of him once, I bet, and given him a thrashing. That looks like a knife wound."

"Shhh," said Doc. "Keep quiet. They're looking right down at us now. Did they see us?"

Tweed pulled back closer to Doc. He shook his head. "No, I don't think they saw us."

Both boys crouched, motionless. It seemed as if the hard beating of their very hearts would betray them. Perspiration dripped down their faces, and Doc's right arm was shaking so badly, that it sounded like a metronome when it touched the statue.

The towering face of the statue above them was frightening enough, but the men in the balcony, stood just as motionless. It seemed to Doc that he and Tweed had been hiding behind the statue for hours, a never-ending nightmare from which he could not awaken. One of the men suddenly cranked his neck and looked sharply toward their hiding place. Had they been seen?

A woman started up the stairs in the direction of the two men. She undoubtedly worked in the building because she wore a nametag. When she reached the top of the stairs, the man with the hat stopped her and asked if there was another stairway on the opposite side of the building. When the woman told them there was, the man lifted his hat, not enough for the boys to see his face, however, and thanked her. Then the pair hurried down the hall to the other staircase.

"Now's our chance," announced Tweed. "C'mon!"

The two boys launched themselves from behind the statue and raced through the door onto the street. They pounded up the street, skidding to a halt near a taxi at the curb.

"We can't risk standing on a corner waiting for a bus," Tweed told Doc. "How much money do you have on you?"

Doc was still shaking too hard to look into his pockets. He was watching behind them.

"Don't worry about it," Tweed then said. "We're a little short, but Grandpa West will pay the balance. This won't be the first time nor probably the last."

Jumping into the cab, the boys told the cabby to hurry as Tweed rattled off his address. As the taxi circled the block, the boys saw the two men standing on a corner looking in every direction. Tweed was about to chuckle when the traffic light turned red. The taxi stopped just as the men turned in their direction.

"Quick, down on the floor!" said Doc, pulling his friend down. "Please lock the doors, Mr. Cab Driver. Those two awful men are after us."

As the driver's head whirled around, the right rear door opened, and the man with the hat stuck his ugly face into the car. He reached for Tweed's collar, but the boy bit his hand, and the thug took a step in retreat. Just then the cabby tromped on the gas, for the light had changed, and the sudden jerk caused the door to slam shut. The two men, jumping up and down and waving their arms, began shouting, but the roaring motor drowned out their words.

"What did those guys want?" asked the cabby.

Doc told him the men had been following them, but he didn't know why. He also said he thought the men were dangerous. The cab driver reached for his phone and called into headquarters. When the dispatcher answered, he told them about the kidnapping attempt and asked the office man to call the police. The man assured him the police would be on the corner in minutes. The cabby asked the boys their names and offered to take them back to the police station. But the boys declined. They wanted to handle this case by themselves. Tweed told him their names were Page and McCloud and that they would telephone a report into the police as soon as they were home.

Doc whispered to Tweed and the other boy nodded.

"You can just drop us off by the Sibley House in Mendota," Tweed told the cab driver, not wanting him to know where he lived.

As the cab sped across the Mendota Bridge and turned onto Highway 13, Tweed told the driver to stop at the bottom of the hill. He was a bit afraid they would be short on the fare, which would necessitate a visit to Grandfather West, but Doc paid it with two dollars to spare.

As they left the taxi and started up the hill, Tweed whispered to Doc, "We've got a problem. My wallet's missing."

Doc turned to him, his eyes wide.

Tweed said, "It's not in my pocket. I didn't want to say anything in front of the driver, and I'm just so happy you had enough money to carry us. I'll pay you back."

"Do you think *they*'ve got it?" Doc asked, again fearful.

Tweed drew in a long breath. "I don't know. I don't know if I dropped it behind the statue or while we were running or if it fell out when he grabbed me. I just hope those crooks don't find my wallet. I have cards in it with my address. I bet I lost it behind the statue."

27

It was just getting dark when the boys reached Tweed's house. Grandfather West was already asleep. He often retired early after fishing all day. Tweed cooked a good supper of bacon, lettuce, and tomato sandwiches and some homemade beef stew.

After they had wolfed down their meal, the boys went into the living room and discussed their day in the city. Doc was staying with Tweed that night, so they talked for nearly three hours. As Tweed was about to shut the light off and head up to bed, he heard a car stop in front of the house. When he heard a door slam, he moved towards the window just as glass exploded in his face and a rock sailed past his head, knocking over and breaking the lamp.

Doc leaped to his feet and helped his friend up.

"Are you okay, Tweed?" he asked, removing some of the glass from his friend's clothing.

"I think so," Tweed said, "but grandfather's window sure isn't. Nor the lamp. Who . . . why?"

Just then Doc reached over and picked up the rock that had been hurled through the window. Tied to the rock was a piece of white paper.

He held it up so Tweed could see it.

The string was tied very tight, and wrapped around the rock several times, but Doc finally managed to loosen it.

Handing the piece of paper to Tweed, he said, "Maybe you want to open this. It is your window they broke, but I have a sneaking suspicion that someone other than the authorities found your wallet. I hope I'm wrong."

Tweed opened the piece of paper, read the note and handed it to Doc. "I think you're right," he muttered.

Doc took the note and held it up to the light coming in from the adjacent room. Out loud he read the words:

"Stay away from Pig's-Eye Cave if you know what's good for you!"

Chapter Three

horse sense

When Grandfather West got up following the broken glass, Tweed and Doc decided to tell him everything, including about the mysterious rowboat and the disappearing head at Fountain Cave. Tweed did state, however, that he was not certain whether the cave incident had any bearing on the kidnapping attempt. In the morning, Grandfather West wisely marched the two boys down to City Hall to report the kidnapping attempt and the broken window.

"Have you ever seen either of those men before?" inquired Sergeant Riley of the St. Paul Police, a tall, balding man with heavy glasses and a thin mustache.

"Never!" both boys answered simultaneously.

Tweed described the two men, especially the man in the slouch hat who had tried to pull him out of the taxi. The sergeant then had the boys look through several books of mug shots in an effort to identify their assailants should they already be known criminals. Although the boys could not be absolutely sure, they agreed that none of the faces shown to them belonged to their pursuers. When they left police headquarters, Sergeant Riley assured them that his men would patrol the Fountain Cave area and keep their eyes open downtown as well. If anything should turn up, Grandfather West would be telephoned with the information. The police also warned the boys to do exactly what the note said, "Stay away from those caves!"

They finally left the station after nearly two hours. As their car progressed down West Seventh Street, Tweed said to Doc, "I'm glad we told them everything, I guess. I wanted to solve this case ourselves, but it turned out to be too dangerous. Anyway, we don't know for absolute sure that those two guys had anything to do with Pig's-Eye Cave. Maybe those guys were just a couple of drunks out looking for trouble. A couple of muggers."

Doc agreed that was possible, but that meant that maybe more people were after them. Still, it felt good to be off the case. His visit had only begun. There would be plenty of time for other adventures. But, though Grandfather West agreed they hadn't done anything to get themselves into trouble, it sure had found them in a hurry.

Tweed's grandfather dropped the boys off at Doc's sister's house in St. Paul. Elizabeth's husband, Andy, had promised to take them to the polo game at Fort Snelling that afternoon. Andy, about twenty-five years old, had a lot of fun with the boys. Though he was a married adult with responsibilities and obligations, he was one of those men who never quite grew up and was willing to chuck all the adult stuff once in a while. He had been a pretty fair polo player himself until a horse had fallen on him during an exhibition match. That made him walk with a cane but hadn't dampened his love for the game.

Andy had a pen full of pigeons in his backyard, and, much to Elizabeth's chagrin, he also had an aquarium full of gecko lizards as pets that he kept in his den. Because of his injury and disability payments, he did not have to work, although he often helped Elizabeth with the household chores. Besides his pigeons and lizards, he loved reading and particularly enjoyed the horror stories of H.P. Lovecraft and Edgar Allan Poe. It had been Andy who turned Doc onto the Doc Savage novels.

After a hasty lunch at the Deckers, Andy and the boys said good-bye to Elizabeth and drove off to the Fort Snelling polo grounds. They reached the field only minutes before game time. Seeing the Fort Snelling team on the sidelines, Andy told the boys he would introduce them to the team.

Tweed had never seen a polo match. Andy explained it. "The game's played on horseback between two teams of four players. The players use mallets with long flexible handles to drive the wooden ball down the field and between the goalposts."

"It sounds pretty dangerous to me," said Tweed. "Don't the horses freak out with all those sticks waving about?"

Andy laughed. "The horses are used to it.Actually it's a pretty safe sport," Andy assured him, "although accidents do happen." With this he lifted his cane into the air, then brought it down to pat his knee. "I guess I know that as well as anyone."

Just then they reached the team, and a couple of the players who were former teammates of Andy's came over to him and shook hands.

"Doc and Tweed, this is Bob Markham, who plays the number one position," said Andy, introducing the boys to a husky young man with a smile that completely covered the lower part of his face. "Each player is given a position with certain responsibilities. No offense, Bob, but the number one player is usually the novice or weakest player on the team. Yet, Bob's position is one of the most difficult to play. He has to be tough—and just look at those muscles—because he is responsible for scoring goals and neutralizing the opposing number four defensive player."

Bob Markham laughed. "Don't believe him," he jested. "It's not all that tough."

Andy then introduced the boys to David Goldman, the number two player. "It's David's job to be the hustler or scrambler, and he must continually scrap for the ball," said Andy.

The number three player, Ed Wilks, was the quarterback or pivot man. "He's a long, powerful hitter and our tactical leader," added Goldman.

Standing nearby was the number four player, Walker Fischer, who had come to America from England. "Walker is our best defensive player," said Goldman.

Andy and the boys talked with the players for a few more minutes before the whistle blew, letting the players know it was time to get ready and everyone else should leave the field. The Sioux Falls team had already assembled on the field as Andy and the boys ran back to join the crowd of spectators on the grass. It was a beautiful sunny day, and if there was anything in the world that could get the boys' minds off their nightmare experience, it was the game of polo.

The two teams of four lined up facing each other in the center of the field. As the referee watched closely from the sidelines, one of the two mounted umpires on the field bowled the ball between the teams. At first it was difficult to tell which team really controlled the ball as horses on both sides sped up and down the field, maneuvering and passing to their fellow players.

"This is the first of six periods in the game," Andy told the boys. "Each period is seven and one-half minutes long. These periods are called 'chukkers,' 'chukkars,' or sometimes 'chukkas.' Here we play six periods, but in Argentina they play eight. Europe plays four."

The boys were held spellbound, watching first one team gallop down the field and attempt to score, and then the other. Mallets clashes, horses wheeled and shouldered each other, and riders shouted encouragement to their mounts. There were not a lot of shots on goal as there was in ice hockey, but when one was attempted, there was a great deal of excitement. After two periods, neither team had scored.

Midway through the third chukker, the local team just missed a scoring opportunity. As the enthusiastic crowd let out a booming, "Ooh," Doc's eyes canvassed the crowd. There were probably close to a hundred spectators, and there were very few who weren't cheering after the near goal.

Suddenly Doc's froze where he sat. At first he couldn't move or speak. He found it impossible to swallow. Then he ducked down behind the woman sitting next to him.

He fumbled for Tweed's sleeve. "T-T-Tweed," he stammered, pointing into the maze of faces with a shaking finger. "O-O-Over there! It's him!"

"It's who?" asked Tweed, turning reluctantly from the field to see what was wrong with Doc. Then he saw Doc's ashen face and looked where he was pointing.

"Look!" said Doc swallowing hard. "Slouch Hat man who tried to kidnap us. It's him talking to those two kids."

Tweed bolted to his feet in surprise. Quickly sitting down, he scanned the area where Doc indicated. "You're right. It's him. What's he doing here? Why's he talking to those two boys? Do you suppose they're his sons?"

"I don't know, Tweed, but they're sure talking a mile a minute. If that one kid shakes his head one more time, I think it'll fall off."

"I think the best thing we can do now is just stay out of sight and keep watch on them. Don't say anything to your Uncle Andy yet until we have a better idea of what is going on."

33

During the fourth chukker, the Fort Snelling club scored on a thrilling long shot by Ed Wilks, giving the team the first point in the match. The boys, however, had trouble keeping their concentration on the game. Twice during that period, two or three boys walked over to the slouch-hatted man and sat down. Both times, the boys who had been sitting there, got up and walked away.

"If they're *all* his kids," hissed Tweed, "he has a mighty big family. He seems to be telling all those kids stuff like he's their boss or something. It's like they come to him for information, and then they leave to do what he said."

"I suppose we could try following a couple of them, but if we get up, old Slouch Hat is going to see us," Doc said.

"Right now I think we should just stay put. Remember we're off this case as amateur detectives. Or are we?"

"I'm itching to clout old Slouch once or twice not only for the chase downtown but for your broken window as well. But maybe we should let Uncle Andy handle this. I'm sure he'd give him a piece of his mind and a piece of his cane. I bet Andy could get some answers out of him."

During the final minutes of the fifth period, Sioux Falls tied the score. Only one boy had joined Slouch Hat during the chukker, and it was quite apparent that neither man nor boy was all that interested in the polo match. While everyone else's face in the audience revealed a look of chagrin over the opponent's goal, Slouch and his young friend showed little interest.

Between the fifth and sixth chukkers, the boys decided to tell Uncle Andy about old Slouch Hat. They knew there would be a scene, but if they could catch him and hold him for the police, they could find out what all their earlier troubles were all about.

"I hate to spoil the game for your Uncle Andy," said Tweed, "but here goes . . ."

34

In hushed tones, the boys told Doc's uncle that old Slouch Hat was sitting in the audience. As the boys pointed him out, Andy rose to his feet. With his cane flying up and down sword-like in the air, he started after the villain. The boys followed close behind him, and although Andy walked with a slight limp, they had trouble keeping up with him.

Slouch Hat did not notice the trio until Andy's cane poked him in the chest. As he stumbled to get up, his young companion dashed away, leaving him alone to face Doc's angry uncle.

"I want some answers, and I want them quick," said Andy, directing his venom at the startled crook. But the man broke away and began running through the crowd, not caring who he knocked over as he pushed his way forward. Because of the cane, Andy could not catch the fleeing villain, but the boys stuck to him like glue.

"If he goes for his car, get his license number," shouted Tweed loud enough for the fleeing man to hear. He hoped in doing so that he could keep the man from going for his car, afraid that his license number would give him. "Now who's chasing who," bellowed Doc after the fleeing man.

The boys' plan worked. Instead of going for his car, Slouch Hat grabbed a bicycle and pedaled off in the direction of Old Fort Snelling.

"Now we can add bicycle theft to the charges," shouted Doc, as the man began making good his escape.

But Uncle Andy had not given up the chase. Hobbling to the sidelines, he got the attention of the Fort Snelling Polo Club's coach, John Stevens. Within minutes, his old buddy Stevens was helping him onto one of the horses on the sidelines. Drawing the reins in his grip, the former polo player was off after the fleeing bicycle thief.

"His name's Flash," shouted Coach Stevens. "Treat him gentle, and you'll think you're riding a bolt of lightning."

Doc and Tweed chuckled in astonishment over the unbelievable chase scene. Retreating was the crook on a stolen bicycle being chased by a lame man on a borrowed horse.

"On, Flash," yelled Andy, his hands cupped around his mouth.

The chase progressed across the parking lot near the old fort with Andy and his mount keeping to the grass, careful not to injure the horse's hooves by forcing him to run on pavement. Slouch Hat was pedaling at full speed, gaining a little lead by taking a diagonal route across the pavement. People getting in and out of cars gaped at the unusual scene as they watched.

Riding the perimeter of the lot, Andy urged Flash forward to make up for lost ground. Just as horse and rider

crossed a sidewalk, a young couple stepped into their path. Andy screamed for them to get back as he and the horse leaped a garbage can and dashed across the pavement. Although the couple was not injured, the jump was anything but perfect. Flash's rear right foot hit the can and sent it spinning across the pavement in the opposite direction. Still, for a polo horse, it was a pretty good effort.

As Andy and Flash approached the old fort, Slouch Hat had already sped by the four original structures—the Round Tower, the Hexagonal Tower, the Officers' Quarters, and the Commandant's House. Slouch Hat probably didn't care that these buildings were the oldest in the state of Minnesota, didn't care about their historical importance; his only interest seemed to be in reaching the woods.

He looked behind himself now and then, probably aghast when he saw again a cloud of dust as his pursuer galloped after him. Whenever the horse crossed a blacktopped sidewalk, the loud cloppity-clop drew the man's attention, and he looked back. The Argentine pony first had been trained as a cow horse, and at age five, retrained for playing polo. Polo ponies reached their peak at about the age of nine, and although Flash had not reached full maturity, he moved with a natural gait.

Andy's saddle was of English-styling, as required for the sport, with a deep seat, like a jumping saddle. Flash's front legs were bandaged from just below the knee to the ankle to prevent injury, but the pony's mane had not been clipped as was usual, and his tail wasn't braided so as not to interfere with players' mallet swing. He was only a back-up horse for this match.

But it was a cane, not a mallet that Andy swung at the man on the bicycle. As Slouch Hat sped down a rough dirt trail that would take him into the state park, he was nearly thrown from the bicycle. The rough path was pocketed with holes, and the handlebars rocked back and forth despite the rider's efforts to stay on course. The man was no mountain biker and started to slow. Flash took the steep hill in stride.

Above both riders loomed the ragged bluffs of Platteville limestone and white sandstone. In front of them stood white birch and other deciduous trees, and beyond, the blue swath of the Minnesota River. But Slouch Hat stayed to the trail paralleling the river with Snelling Lake on his other side.

Although on foot, Tweed and Doc had traversed the parking lot and run as far as the wall encircling the fort. Below them, they could see the strange duo—a galloping polo horse and a stolen bicycle—speeding through a ravine past red oaks and tall grass. The boys descended the hill.

At the edge of the lake, Andy Decker caught up to his quarry. In a feat of Wild West action, he pulled alongside the bicyclist and jarred him with his cane. When the man in the hat refused to stop, Uncle Decker leaped from Flash's back onto the back of his adversary. The bicycle careened into a tree, the crash throwing both men to the ground.

Dazed, Andy staggered to his feet and pounced again on the man. With a right hook, he knocked the man down, then pulled him back up to give him more of the same. But the mystery man was not finished. Blocking the next blow, he placed his foot behind Andy's leg and pushed him backward. Andy fell into the dirt as the man hammered him with fists of steel.

Grabbing the man's fists, Andy gradually pushed the man off him. Instead of coming back at Andy, the man rushed to the polo horse Flash, standing nearby. Reaching into the pouch on the horse's side, he withdrew a polo mallet and advanced on Andy as he was getting to his feet.

Just as he was about to bring the mallet down on Andy's head, voices bellowed "Stop!"

Dropping the mallet, the scared villain looked up to see the two boys running down the road at him. Quickly, Slouch

Hat ran to the horse and leaped upon his back. Slapping the animal's rear, the man pressed the horse into a gallop toward the boys.

Tweed and Doc froze in their tracks. They clearly had not expected this turn of events. They were about to be trampled!

Chapter Four

crash dive

Slouch Hat, mounted on Flash, charged the two boys. Just as the horse's hooves seemed about to come down on their heads, Tweed pushed Doc to one side and fell on top of him, narrowly missing being trampled to death. The excited horse came to an abrupt halt, throwing Slouch Hat—his arms and legs flailing—several feet into the air. Slouch Hat landed on a part of his anatomy where it hurt the least, scrambled to his feet, and charged into the woods. It was impossible to tell whether he had been hurt by his sudden fall.

"Let him go." Uncle Andy limped up to the boys and helped them to their feet. He made certain they had not been injured, then sat down at the edge of the path. "I'm just too plain pooped to pop, and he has a pretty good head start on us already. Besides, we'd never find that rascal in those woods on foot and we really should take Flash back to Coach Stevens and its owner."

"Sure, Andy," said Doc, glad to be safe again. He worked at bringing what felt like hyperventilation back to normal breathing. "I think that's enough excitement for one day. I only hope we've seen the last of him."

Tweed was looking to the woods where the man had disappeared. "Somehow, I don't think we have," he said, brushing dirt from his pants. "We either know too much about their operation, or we've got something they want."

"But we don't know anything about their operation," Doc said. "We don't know anything. And we haven't got anything either."

"Look, boys," said Andy, holding Flash's reins and attempting to steady him. "You know something is up at that cave. That is a good start, but I suggest you let the police handle the situation from here on. It's beginning to get dangerous."

"But, gee, Andy," said Tweed, "that's what mysteries are all about. There's always an element of danger, or it wouldn't be a mystery."

Andy's expression showed no humor. "Oh, I know, but two fourteen-year-old boys I know need to know when to quit. The police must be brought in. That man is dangerous." Then he winked, "Look, I can't tell you it's okay to do anything, and I won't, but I know you two and your buddy."

Doc and Tweed exchanged looks. Doc said, "What buddy?"

"Trouble. The three of you link forces every summer. You've been together a couple of days, and already we've been to the police station and got into a fight that could have gone very badly."

"Wait a minute," said Doc. "*You* got into the fight."

Andy chuckled and rubbed his chin. "So I did. As one of Trouble's older buddies, let me say this. If you boys insist on following up your clues, I suggest you do it only from a safe distance. You see that guy or his friend again, you go to the police straight away. Promise me that."

Doc said, "But that is all we have *been* doing."

"Wrong," Andy replied. "I said observe from a *safe* distance. Climbing about those rocks over the cave was *not* a safe distance. You need to watch it from a long way's off, from somewhere they would never suspect. Surveillance from far away yet close to the action."

"But there is no such place," countered Tweed with a long face. We only had two places to watch them from, and we tried both. We checked out the cave area from the boat and then climbed down from above."

Andy's eyes twinkled. "Ah, but there's a way of being right on top of them without them even knowing it. A place you've obviously overlooked. And it is safer than either of the ways you have already tried."

"Where?" cried both boys in unison.

"From above!"

Tweed looked almost cross-eyed in befuddlement. "From above . . . where?"

Andy chuckled, obviously have a good time with them. "You'd be smack dab over the middle of the Mississippi River looking right down at Pig's Eye Cave. If anything so much as moved an inch, you'd see it. And maybe it'd show where the entrance to the cave is, that is, if there is an entrance."

"I just don't understand, Andy," replied Tweed. "I suppose we might try making our own hang glider, but that'd take us the rest of Doc's stay."

Doc, looking down-hearted, said, "You're trying to convince us to find some other adventure, right?"

42

Andy shook his head, then pointed up river with his chin. "Look there. What do you see?"

Doc and Tweed looked up the river, seeing very little that would help. Even if they could get really powerful binoculars, Doc knew no place on the bluffs that gave a vantage of the cave. He doubted Tweed knew one either. Then he saw it, and his eyes slid back up to his uncle's smiling face. "The balloon?" he asked without conviction.

Andy laughed when Tweed also looked hopeless. Andy said, "My good friend Corky Reynolds owns that very hot air balloon and takes people up in it every decent day from Harriet Island. I bet I could get him to give two boys needing to get a bird's eye view of Pig's Eye a real deal. In fact, if you two will promise to stay away from that place and those men, I'll call him as soon as we get back to Fort Snelling with Flash and that bicycle. That is, if you boys aren't afraid to fly. . . ."

"Golly, no," said Doc, struggling to get the words out around his growing excitement. "I'll go up if Tweed will. It isn't every day a kid gets to go up in a hot air balloon."

"Agree!" said Tweed. He didn't look a bit scared.

"The balloon is safer than everything you've already attempted. But before we call Corky, I want to clear all this with Grampa West and make sure he gives his permission for you to launch yourselves into the stratosphere. But I don't really foresee any problems there. He knows what the two of you are like when you get together."

The trio returned Flash to its owner and drove to Grampa West's home. Mr. West could see no reason why the boys shouldn't go up in the hot air balloon with Mr. Reynolds and told Andy that, had he been a bit younger, he'd have liked to accompany them. Andy telephoned Corky Reynolds, and the balloonist agreed to take the boys up at ten o'clock the following morning if the weather allowed.

Doc was again staying with Tweed that night, but truthfully neither boy slept much.

The morning dawned clear and sunny as the boys gobbled down their breakfast of cereal and toast. They listened to the weather report tensely, then relaxed a little when the Channel Eleven weatherman said winds would be light and no rain or storms were expected for at least two days. Just as they took their last bite of toast with grape jelly, they heard Andy's familiar "honk" outside, and both boys made a bee-line for the door.

"Not so fast, young men," interjected Grampa West, giving them his most serious expression. "Don't try anything silly up in that balloon, you understand? Hot air balloons are perfectly safe if you follow the rules, so follow them. Be sure you're courteous to Mr. Reynolds, too. This is awfully nice of him to take you boys up for nothing when he could be making a few bucks taking up others in that time slot."

The boys agreed, thanked Grampa West, and tore out the door. Within minutes, they were speeding along Highway 13 and winding down the long hill past the Lilydale Yacht Club. The ride through the beautiful regional park passed quickly, and, truthfully, neither boy saw much of it, focusing so hard, as they were, on the adventure ahead of them. Across the river they could see the blinking light of the Northern States Power Company as well as the ugly storage tanks and drawbridge skirting the shore.

Just before reaching Harriet Island, they gazed at the numerous caves to their immediate right, caverns turned into storage garages. Once many of these caves on the right side of the Mississippi served as gangster hangouts, and one in particular, was a 1930s nightclub frequented by the likes of Alvin "Creepy" Karpis, "Ma" Barker's infamous sons—Fred and Doc—and maybe even Al Capone.

"That's Harriet Island just ahead of us," Andy said, pointing to an open area along the riverbank. "Way back before my time, the island was known for its famous public baths. Later it became a marina. It's not really an island, though, but Navy Island is just off shore. You get to it over a small bridge. And, look," said Andy, pointing slightly down the river, "you can see about where Pig's-Eye Cave is. Up in the balloon, you'll have a great view."

Corky Reynolds, a short, thin man barely taller than Tweed, had a wide smile, crinkled blue eyes, and a fisherman's cap worn at the back of his head. He was waiting for them as they parked their car. After introductions, Andy, who had some shopping to do in St. Paul, drove away. He'd pick up the boys in a couple hours. Corky ushered them toward the multi-colored balloon that lay waiting for them at the edge of the river, looking like some deflated tent. Doc thought the balloon's carriage resembled a large Easter basket he had once made for his mother.

"How does it stay up, Mr. Reynolds?" inquired a nervous Tweed Salter, fidgeting with a camera he had brought along for the aerial excursion.

The man grinned. "First of all, boys, no more of this Mr. Reynolds stuff. My friends call me Corky."

Doc wondered about his real first name—probably Corcoran or something equally distasteful—but he said boldly, "Okay, Corky."

"There's a little basic physics involved in hot air balloon travel, boys, and it's kind of complicated," said Corky. "It has to do with the effect of increased temperature on the motions of molecules of a gas, as well as on their density. I am afraid you'd have to know a little bit about thermodynamics for a good explanation."

"Uh . . . thermo . . . what?" gulped Doc.

45

Corky chuckled and motioned to the boys to come aboard. Doc and Tweed climbed into the basket. The little man hopped in after them and turned on a large flame attached to two silver cylinders of propane. The roar was rather frightening, and the boys cringed.

Corky laughed jovially. In nearly a shout and with hand motions to clarify what he meant, he said, "In order for our balloon to lift off, it must be lighter than an equal volume of the air around it. A hot air balloon stays afloat in the cooler air around it due to the buoyant force on it. Think of yourselves in a pool of water. Ever notice that it is much easier to lift someone when you are both in the water?"

Both boys nodded.

Corky grinned wider and said, "That's because of the partial support the water is offering the buoyant force."

Just then, the boys noticed they were about to leave the ground. The great envelope had billowed, slowly filling with hot air from the flame jets. It kind of righted itself over the basket, looking a little egg shaped and squashed, then filled. It tugged at the tethers, and the basket tottered. Both boys gripped the sides. Doc felt a sudden impulse to climb over the side and jump out, but he didn't. He watched the flame jets fill the envelope another moment. Then he looked down to see they were already well off the ground.

Corky suddenly turned off the gas jets, and the flames vanished. In a normal voice, he said, "Forget all the algebra and physics, boys. Hot air rises. It's just that simple. Enjoy the ride."

Still rising, they were now drifting off over the muddy Mississippi. Having overcome their fear, both boys began to revel in the odyssey and their amazing view. "It is almost like flying without wings," interjected Tweed, still twirling his camera strap around his wrist.

To the southwest they could see the High Bridge and barely catch a glimpse of the tip of Pike Island, where the Minnesota River emptied into the Mississippi. In the opposite direction, they watched a passenger train slowly snake past Dayton's Bluff and what had once been Carver's Cave.

"From what Andy said, you want me to hover over the river just this side of Pig's Eye Cave. Is that right, boys?" asked Corky.

"Yes, sir," replied Tweed, who then commenced to tell Corky everything that had happened since their initial visit to the cave site.

"It does sound like those creeps are up to something," said Corky. "Andy told me the police are also looking into it."

The balloon seemed to freeze in mid-air, high above the river. Looking down several hundred yards, they had a bird's-eye view of the spot above Pig's Eye Cave where they had seen the mysterious man disappear into the rocks. Although there was a car on the parking lot above the cave site, they saw no one now. Neither of the boys had remembered the make and model of the two cars they had seen there earlier so there was no telling if this was one of them, but Doc thought it might have been.

For two hours, nothing happened, as they slowly drifted above the river front. The car had not left the parking lot, though others had come and gone, and they had glimpsed nothing out of the ordinary. Just as Corky was about to call off the vigil for the day, an excited Doc pointed to a section of Shepard Road just west of the cave.

"Look," he exclaimed. "Three kids on bicycles, and they're riding them as fast as their legs will pedal. I think those kids are up to something, and I'll just bet they're headed toward the cave,"

Corky said, "I don't know. They might just be kids following the bike path for a morning ride."

"Maybe," said Doc, a little deflated, "but they're going so fast, it is almost as if they are trying to get away from something."

"Or someone." This was Tweed.

Corky guided the balloon slightly away from the cave so as to throw off any suspicion of their vigilance. The cyclists approached the cave parking lot. Tweed pointed in the opposite direction to a fourth cyclist approaching the cave from the east. Corky and Doc nodded. They had seen this person as well.

The first three boys pulled up at the parking lot as Tweed snapped their picture from the balloon. Looking around them, as if to see if they were being watched, they walked their bikes to the rocks. One of them pointed up at the balloon just before they disappeared into a cleft. Just then the fourth boy arrived and, like the others, walked his bike into the rocks.

"They saw us!" said Doc. "I'm sure they spotted us."

"We don't have to worry about that, boys," said Corky. "I am up here every day, and I'm not the only one. There are several balloonists that give rides along here."

"But they saw us," said Doc again.

"I'm sure they did. But I doubt they thought anything about it. I just wonder where they took those bikes."

"They completely disappeared," remarked Doc.

"Can you bring her down a little closer, Corky?" asked Tweed. "Maybe we can get a little closer look at the place."

"You don't want to get too close, Tweed," cautioned Corky. "Then they *will* get suspicious."

"Here comes another kid down Randolph on a bike," said Doc, pointing. "I bet you a penny he turns onto Shepard Road and heads for the cave."

There were no takers. The boy followed the same course as the others onto Shepard Road and pulled up abruptly in the parking lot. Like the others, he turned to look over his shoulder and scanned the highway as Tweed again snapped a picture. Certain he was not being watched, the boy walked his bike toward the rocks, all the while looking up at the curious balloon floating over the river above him.

49

The trio spent another hour in the balloon, but no more bikers pulled up to the parking lot. Finally all five boys emerged from the cleft *without* their bicycles. They stood staring up at the balloon, holding a hand over their eyes to keep the sun from streaming into their faces. One of the youngsters disappeared back into the cleft while the others remained staring at the balloon.

"I think they're suspicious," said Corky. "I didn't think they'd get wise so fast, but we *have* been here a long time."

The three in the balloon continued to watch the boys in the parking lot. Just then the fifth boy came out of the cleft. All the boys began walking away from Pig's Eye Cave, three headed west down Shepard Road while the other two walked east. Occasionally, one would glance over his shoulder at the balloon.

"They're wise to us, all right," said Corky. "I sure wonder what they did with those bikes. Why on earth would a bunch of kids ride like mad to the cave, then forget their bikes and walk home?"

"I don't know," replied Tweed, "but if you can take this thing down there, we can check it out. Those bikes have to be someplace."

"It isn't as easy as all that, boys," said Corky. "That's a a pretty tough place to bring down a balloon. We could try for the parking lot but that would be dangerous in more ways than one. I think we better return to Harriet Island. Anyway, Andy is probably waiting for us by now. Perhaps the four of us can take a quick drive across the river to Fountain Cave and take a look."

"Wait!" yelled Doc, suddenly alarmed. "Look! There! Those are the two guys who chased us downtown and around the Indian statue. That's the one who was going to hit Andy with a polo mallet!"

Tweed gaped. "Yep, that's definitely old Slouch Hat himself and the other goon to boot." Tweed snapped several pictures of them. He wanted to yell out, "How does it feel to get thrown on your fanny from a horse?" but he kept his cool.

"They're looking up at us and pointing," said Doc, wishing he were anywhere but a passenger in that balloon. He felt vulnerable, exposed, and, with the huge balloon over his head, visible.

"Yeah, I definitely think they know who we are," said Tweed.

"Well," said Corky, "I think they're pretty sure we're up to something. Those kids left those bikes for a reason, and they already suspected you were on to them. That's why they came after you. If they think it's you up here, they might try something worse. I'm bringing the balloon back to Harriet. We'll call the police, and then maybe Andy and I are going to take a little ride over to Pig's Eye Cave."

"But we get to go with, don't we?" This was Doc.

"We certainly won't leave you boys alone. All four of us will go over there. I am sure the police will be there before us anyway."

Tweed got a strange look in his eyes. In a low voice, he said, "Do we have to tell the police? Doc and I really wanted to solve this case by ourselves."

Corky grinned. "You've already solved the case, guys. Those bikes—they have to be stolen—and you know as well as I do that there's a secret entrance to that cave. I think the police can take over from there. But you kids are heroes, and there's probably a reward for information leading to the capture of these thieves. You certainly have earned it."

The two men on the ground were still looking up at them as the balloon drifted away from the Pig's-Eye cave area, and, although there was a great distance between them and the balloon, they appeared to recognize the boys. Tweed thought the duo looked more menacing than ever, and as much as he hated to admit it, he believed that the police could handle these guys a lot better than he and Doc could. They had already proven themselves a little more dangerous than he and Doc liked their summer adventures.

As Corky maneuvered the ship toward Harriet Island, the boys saw Slouch Hat take something from his pocket and hold it up in the air.

"It's a gun," yelled Doc, "and he is pointing it right at us. If he hits our balloon, we . . . no . . . oh, my gosh! We've been hit! We're going to crash!"

Chapter five

midnight mayhem

Tweed Salter laughed and began poking his fist in Doc's stomach. "He didn't shoot at us, you dummy. You're hearing noises from the barges again. Look down there behind us, and you'll see what I mean."

Doc looked where he was told and, seeing the barge, tried not to show his embarrassment. His mouth opened but he did not speak.

Corky was squinting at the man. "I don't think that's a gun he's got aimed at us. Look. He is still pointing it at us. It looks like a spyglass from here. Yep, that's what it is. That wily rascal is watching us through the glass. Now, we know you've been recognized."

Corky directed the balloon in a southeasterly direction toward Harriet Island. As they floated loftily over the river the boys kept their faces glued on their adversaries, who were growing smaller and smaller as the balloon carried them away. Doc, who was often known for his impulsiveness, foolishly waved at the two men. Corky laughed, but Tweed poked Doc hard and shook his head. By waving at the crooks, he was pretty much letting them know they were watching them.

"That settles it," said Tweed. "Now you did it! Now they know it's us in the balloon, and they'll be on guard all the more. Plus, now they'll probably come after us with a real gun."

"I'm sorry," Doc apologized. "I just wasn't thinking. I figured they saw who we were anyway, so I'd just kick a little dirt in their faces."

"Well, I'm afraid we are in for it now," said Tweed. "But at least things are out in the open, and they know we're wise to them. They'll probably clear out before the police can even grab 'em."

Corky brought the balloon down gently on Harriet Island and secured it as the boys climbed out. Andy was waiting. Talking quickly both at once, they told Andy everything that had happened during their aerial surveillance trip. Corky went to his car, grabbed his cell phone and telephoned the police. His assistants took over the aerial tours for the small group of people waiting a turn. Then he and the two boys joined Andy in his car. Within minutes they were driving down Plato Boulevard.

As they crossed the Wabasha Street Bridge over the river, they could see the flashing red and blue lights of three police cars down below on Shepard Road. The police vehicles were moving at a rapid pace, and the boys hoped they would reach Pig's-Eye Cave before the two crooks could make their getaway.

Soon Andy was guiding them down Shepard Road. By the time they reached the cave parking lot, they found only the three police cars with their flashing lights. The officers had scurried onto the rocks and down into the trees and tangled weeds below in an effort to nab their quarry. Andy, Corky, Doc, and Tweed, scampered down what had once been a path between the rocks, now so overgrown with weeds that it was impossible to follow.

"Put your hands up!" demanded a loud, bold voice. As the foursome complied, the boys were certain they had been captured by the crooks.

"Sorry about that, gentlemen," said a friendly police officer. "You startled me for a minute. I thought you might have been the men we're looking for. You best get back up in the parking lot."

Tweed and Doc explained their involvement and showed the officers where the two men had been standing when they

had pointed up at the balloon. Tweed also pointed out the general area where Slouch Hat and the bikers had disappeared. The police covered every inch of ground but turned up no clues, except for some possible footprints too shallow to follow.

"I'm afraid they took off," said Sergeant Berven. "They must have heard us coming here and flew the coop. I'd like you boys to come downtown with me and spend an hour or so looking at mug shots again. Maybe you'll recognize one or both of the men."

The boys agreed, and Doc asked if they could ride in the police car. Sergeant Berven chuckled, glanced at Andy and Corky, and nodded his approval.

"Yippee!" yelled Doc so loud, that, if the crooks were within a mile of the cave, they'd know they had visitors.

A little later, walking up the stairs of the gray, three-story building with the police officers, Doc whispered to Tweed, "It's like we're really detectives now."

Once inside, the boys were greeted by a red-haired desk sergeant, who ushered them up a set of stairs to the Investigative Bureau and down to the Forgery and Theft Division. They were greeted by Captain Daniel Anderson.

"You boys are in for a special treat," said the policeman. "In the past, you'd have had to look through the General Mugshot Catalog. You looked at something like that already. We have dozens of huge three-ring binders. But up here we have everything computerized. You merely sit back and watch them on videos. They are set up by category. You can look at the video of white males, thirty to forty years old."

Captain Anderson led them to a large console television monitor.

"We call this a 'TV with shrouds,'" pointed out the captain, "the shrouds, of course, being visors on the sides of the set to keep out the fluorescent lighting."

Tweed and Doc sat down before the recessed screen while an officer slipped a video or microfilm into the set. Handing the boys a remote, Captain Anderson told the boys to click on the button to change images. Each mugshot had a front and side view, and within minutes, the boys had the hang of it and were clicking at a rapid pace.

The boys spent two hours looking at photographs. Towards the end of their session, all the men were starting to look alike. They were absolutely sure that none of the men pictured were their two adversaries at Pig's-Eye Cave.

"They could be out-of-state men," commented the sergeant. "They may have a racket going in several states and never really stay long in one place. Some of these guys think they can stay a step ahead of the police, but we usually get them in the end."

The boys shook hands with the police officers as they left. Andy, after dropping Corky off at Harriet Island, drove the boys home. Grandfather West was waiting at the door, and Andy and the boys told him everything that had happened.

"Be sure and lock your doors tonight," cautioned Andy, stepping into his car for the ride home. "You never know about those creeps. If they saw you taking pictures of them, they might come looking for you. If you'd like, I can call Sergeant Berven back and have him place an officer near the property here tonight."

"No, thanks, Andy," said Grandfather West. "I'm sure we'll be just fine. And if they do come looking for trouble, we'll be ready for them."

Andy drove away, and Grandpa West told the boys to come inside for something to eat. They did not have to be told twice. Soon they were hungrily devouring cold chicken sandwiches, macaroni and cheese, steamed green beans fresh from the garden, and tall glasses of milk.

"I've been thinking," said the older man. "You kids have been through a lot with these crooks these past few days. Maybe you need a little break. The State Fair starts tomorrow. How about if we spend the day there? While you guys are running around eating Pronto Pups and trying out rides, I'll take in the Hippodrome, Horticulture Building, Natural Resources Building, and maybe the Mexican Village. And, heck, I want to eat that famous chicken at that kitchen there and see some of the new equipment on Machinery Hill. I'll stay out of your way, but we can meet somewhere later in the evening. How does that sound?"

"You've got yourself a deal, Mr. West," cried Doc, while Tweed nodded vigorously in agreement.

The boys spent the remainder of the evening listening to their favorite CDs, a compilation of the latest rock music as well as some oldies. With the darkness came some fear, however, fear that the two thugs might come after them or the film they had taken. Neither boy wanted to mention the possibility of their having a nocturnal visit, but after the last CD finished playing, Doc looked up at Tweed and sputtered, "D-Do ya suppose . . ."

Tweed finished the sentence for him: "that the thugs might show up around here tonight? I don't know. I think it's possible. Perhaps we should take a few precautions just in case."

"Maybe we better wake up your grampa and ask him what to do," said Doc.

"Naw, let Gramps get his sleep. I hate to worry him over something that probably won't happen anyway." Then Tweed brightened. "Follow me outside. I have an idea."

The two boys, accompanied by Mustard, cautiously crept out into the darkness of the yard, looking around carefully and listening for any unusual noise. Tweed dipped into the recycling barrel and produced an armful of empty tin cans. Trying not to awaken Grandfather West, they carried armfuls of cans back inside the house and tied several to the bottom catch of each of the sliding windows. Should the windows be opened during the night, the motion would tug on the rope and rattle the cans.

"Do you think the cans will rattle loud enough for us to hear?" asked Doc. "Seems to me the sound would be pretty soft."

"For us? Probably. But Mustard's ears are a lot better than ours. If there's any sound in any of the rooms, he'll bark. *That* we'll hear for sure."

"Now, I've got an idea," said Doc. "Come on back outside."

"What have you got up your sleeve, o' humble wizard?" jested Tweed.

"Well, we can't do your grandfather's room, but we haven't booby-trapped our bedroom yet. Of course, we should save the best until last."

Stopping on the porch, Doc reached up and removed a set of wind chimes hanging from a hook.

"We'll tie these to the window latch inside our bedroom," he said, proud of himself for coming up with the idea. "If Slouch Hat or his buddy opens our window tonight, they'll get quite a surprise."

"Great thinking, Doc," said Tweed, clapping him on the back. "That'll really make noise should the thugs try to enter that way. With the cops after them, they'd be stupid to show up here, but it is good to be prepared just in case. And I'm gonna take Grandpa's big spotlight to bed with us. If we hear a rumpus, we can shine it right on them."

Satisfied that they had all their bases covered, the boys slipped into their pajamas, closed their bedroom door and hopped into bed. Of course, Mustard lay between them in his accustomed place. Neither boy could fall asleep, though. They studied the shadows within the room over and over, imagining them as hunched-over men or arms with knives raised to strike. Twice Doc got up and peered through the window.

By eleven o'clock, however, they began to get sleepy. Tweed fell off first, and his snoring let Doc know that his friend no longer worried about the men from Pig's Eye. He, growing groggy, tried to keep one eye open for at least another hour after Tweed had fallen asleep.

Mustard woofed. Tweed woke up at once. It was after midnight. He asked Doc if he had heard anything, but his friend from Illinois had finally fallen asleep and did not answer.

A loud clanging came from the yard outside their window. Mustard growled. Tweed shook Doc, whose eyes flew open. Tweed held his hand over Doc's mouth and crossed his own lips with a finger. Both Doc and Tweed slipped out of bed and slowly crept toward the window.

The yard was pitch black except for the yard light on the opposite side of the house, which created sinister shadows in the semi-darkness. Both boys stared into the blackness, but they saw nothing.

"I know I heard a loud bang," whispered Tweed. "I'm sure of it."

"Me, too," replied Doc. "I was sound asleep, and it woke me up. I think I heard Mustard, too, but that might have been in my dream."

Suddenly something moved in the shadow of the garage and slinked off into a corner where the dim light could not penetrate. It had moved quickly and quietly, and then all was still.

"Did you see that?" asked Tweed, his lips beginning to tremble.

"I wish I hadn't, but I did," answered Doc. "We should have let Andy post an officer out here. Something . . . that is, some*body*'s definitely out there, and he's watching us."

Once Doc thought he saw another movement in the darkness, but he wasn't sure. Tweed picked up the phone on the nightstand by his bed and held it in his hand.

"If I see someone for sure, I'm calling 911. I'm scared these guys mean business, and we don't know what they're up to."

Suddenly, there was another loud banging followed by a sliding or rolling sound. Then another and another. Mustard began to bark fiercely, and Doc quickly placed his hand around the dog's mouth. "Nice boy," he whispered. "Sh-hh!"

Both boys were mesmerized. Tweed considering opening the window (which he hoped would scare the intruders away) and turning the powerful flashlight on them. He looked down at the phone in his hands and pushed the nine and a one, but then he paused.

Just as he had decided he really should push the last one, a large raccoon followed by four of her cubs strolled out into the moonlight. They waddled in the direction of the porch, sniffed the air, and passed into the shadows.

Tweed hung up the phone. "The garbage can," he said with relief, and poked Doc in the ribs. In a minute he was laughing. "They knocked it over and were sifting through its contents on the ground."

"Some detective you are," teased Doc. "You thought it was the Pig's-Eye pair for sure, and you were darned scared."

"So were you. You were *twice* as scared as I was."

"Was not!"

"Was too!"

The boys laughed and wrestled on the floor, each insisting they weren't completely fooled by the animal visitors.

Tweed rolled onto his back and looked up at the ceiling. "Gosh, it's late. We have to get some sleep if we're going with Grampa to the fair in the morning and be awake to enjoy anything."

"I hate to tell you this, but it's already morning," said Doc, pointing at the clock, which read quarter to three. "We can still get a little sleep if we stop worrying about those dummies in the cave. I'll probably dream about raccoons instead."

The boys chuckled, talked for fifteen minutes, then fell asleep. Mustard curled up at their feet and kept vigil on the window. Having seen raccoons on his turf excited him, and unlike the boys, he was ready for action.

A small cloud passed over the moon, obscuring what little light it had cast. The yard light around back continued its eerie glow. A lingering silence fell over the house, and except for an occasional truck roaring down Highway 110, all was quiet. Too quiet.

Mustard began to growl, and he stood up on the bed and began wagging his tail. His was a quiet warning, however. Because both boys were bushed, neither woke. Mustard held his ground, content in knowing he was protecting his master.

Without another warning, the window in the boys' bedroom was raised, and the wind chimes clanged together in what sounded like loud oriental music. Both boys sat up with a start, and Tweed fumbled in the dark for the flashlight. His fingers found it wedged between the pillows, and he aimed it at the window and clicked it on. Silhouetted in its wide, bright beam was a menacing, very large face, bearing a hideous scar on the left cheek.

"Gimme the film," bellowed the man in a gruff voice, "or it'll be curtains for you!"

fair play

Both boys screamed in unison, but Mustard, not to be out-done by Lassie or Rin Tin Tin regardless of their considerably larger size, rushed across the room and dove into the face of the intruder, knocking him down. As the startled burglar wrestled on the ground with the wily little dog outside the bedroom window, Grandpa West came into the boys' room to see what all the fuss was about.

"It was Scarface!" shouted Tweed. "It's one of the men from the cave. He tried to come in, but Mustard tackled him through the window."

Grandpa ran to the window, only to see Mustard return-ing from a chase through the garden. There were definite signs of a scuffle on the ground below the window. Mustard had a piece of fabric in his mouth, and he shook it vigorously.

"One thing's for certain," chuckled Grandpa. "That crook'll have a somewhat cold behind. Looks like Mustard ripped out the seat of his pants. I'm going to keep that for the police. It may be a clue. Hand me your phone, Tweed. I am going to call the police right now."

The police arrived twenty minutes later, surveying the ground where Mustard had fought with the burglar and checking for finger prints on the window sill.

"Pretty clever how you boys rigged up all those booby traps," said the officer in charge with a wink, "but for the next several nights I'm going to post an officer outside your house, Mr. West. You won't need those traps. Officer Baardson here knows his stuff. He'll keep a keen lookout should those robbers return."

It was 4:00 a.m. before the police finished dusting for fingerprints and concluding their questioning. Both boys were exhausted although Grandfather West seemed too wired to sleep.

"You boys better get back to bed," he told them. "We'll be leaving for the fair in a few hours. We'll make a day of it. It'll help keep your mind off those hoodlums. Of course, you have to promise to watch your step at the fair."

"We'll recognize Scarface and Slouch Hat if they show up there, Grandpa," piped Tweed. "I think Mustard should get an extra dog treat tonight. He saved our bacon."

"I'll get Mustard his treat. Off with you, now. We'll talk about all this tomorrow," said Grandpa.

The morning dawned bright and sunny. It felt to Doc and Tweed as if they had just lowered their heads to their pillows, but sunshine streamed through the window. With the shadows gone, so did much of their fears. Grandfather West called to them as if he had already done so several times, "Flapjacks! Come and get 'em while they're hot."

Doc was dressed before Tweed could get to his feet. The strong aroma of bacon, eggs, and pancakes filled the room. By the time Tweed moped his way into the kitchen, Doc had already devoured a stack of flapjacks and a healthy portion of his eggs and bacon.

"Nice of you to save some for me," joked Tweed, taking his place at the table.

"There's plenty more where those came from, Tweed," said Grandpa with a smile. "Eat up so we can get off to the fair."

The ride down the interstate seemed to take only minutes, and it was not until the trio reached the corner of Snelling and Como that they were stuck dead in traffic heading to the fair. Grandpa, however, wheeled into a lot on Como Avenue and parked. Before the older man was even out of the car, the boys were running toward the bridge that crossed over the highway to the fairgrounds. Grandpa West whistled loudly, and both boys stopped and turned. He waved several dollar bills in his hand. The boys galloped back to him.

"We'll meet you in front of the grandstand about seven o'clock, Grandpa," said Tweed as he pocketed the money. "Then maybe we can all watch the fireworks together before we go home."

As the boys dashed off again, Grandpa West called after them, "Don't eat all the Pronto Pups!"

Within minutes the boys walked down Commonwealth Avenue, each chewing a foot long hotdog while popping in some cheese curds as if they hadn't just eaten a large breakfast not one hour earlier. They strolled through the Grandstand, ate cotton candy at the band shell, bought more hot dogs at Baldwin Park, and took in the exhibits at Heritage Square. Along the way they stopped to watch the State Fair Mall Parade as it wound its way over a fourteen-block route beginning and ending at the corner of Judson and Underwood. While they thoroughly enjoyed colorful floats, animals, specialty acts, and visiting royalty from festivals throughout the state, they were especially enthralled by the high school marching band competition. In between the consumption of Pronto Pups and Lebanese pocket sandwiches, they caught the end of the annual eight-k run which began and ended in the Grandstand infield.

But, even though eating seemed to be their focus, the enthusiastic boys had come to the fair with one thing in mind, and it wasn't the fair food. After a perfunctory tour of the grounds and considerable munching along the way, they headed for their favorite place at the fair: The Midway. Dashing down the street, weaving in and out of crowds of fair-goers, they headed straight for the roller coaster. As they stood waiting to board the "Scream Machine," Tweed had the opportunity to share with his friend a bit of history.

"Did you know that the first roller coasters were made in Russia during the 1600s?"

"You're kidding, of course," said Doc.

"Nope. They shaped blocks of ice into sleds and used straw or fur on the ice as seats to keep people from freezing. They used sand at the end to keep people from crashing. It made for quite the fast ride . . . not too safe, though."

Their turn came, and suddenly they were flying down the track of the tubular coaster at sixty miles per hour, grimacing at hairpin turns and death-defying loops and screaming with everyone else on the steep downhill races.

"I think my heart's in my stomach," yelled Doc, tugging on his safety harness as the roller coaster climbed yet another hill.

"You can't fall out," said Tweed. "The coaster has no engine. We were pulled up to the top of the first hill, but after that the coaster completes the rest of the ride on its own. That's why they call it a *coaster*."

Doc cringed as they dropped down the steepest slope yet and roared around another hairpin turn.

"You and your physics," he shouted earnestly.

Just as the coaster slowed for the end of the ride to allow the boys to catch their breaths, Doc pointed to two men standing near the ticket booth far below them.

"Tweed, look! It's . . . It's . . . them!"

"You're right." Tweed's voice choked with fear. "It's Slouch Hat and Scarface, and they're watching us."

"But how did they know we were here?"

"I don't know. I don't think they'd dare try anything here in front of thousands of people. We have to act like we haven't seen them and stay away from anyplace where there aren't a lot of people. We'll catch a couple more rides and act as if nothing's up. Smile, Doc, laugh even. Oh, no! They're coming."

As the boys exited the coaster, they saw Scarface come around the ride to their left, while his companion remained on their right.

"Maybe we can lose them in the crowd," said Tweed in a harsh whisper. "But don't run. We don't want them to know we're on to them."

The frightened boys walked quickly across the crowded Midway, but, despite their dodging in and out of groups of people, their pursuers kept pace.

"The bumper cars," whispered Tweed. "There's hardly any line. We'll grab a couple cars and just pretend they don't exist. Maybe they'll get careless and lose track of us. It's worth a try."

"I don't think they came here to forget about us, Tweed," said Doc with feeling, "but, who knows? It might work, and they certainly can't grab us in there. Maybe your grandpa will come looking for us."

Purchasing tickets, the boys dashed into the arena. Each climbed into a bumper car. Tweed looked above him, his eyes following the pole which carried the electricity to the car from the iron grid in the ceiling, hoping that the ride would begin.

"Don't look now," cautioned Doc, "but those two thugs just bought tickets. They're going to ride bumper cars with us!"

Tweed had frozen. He swallowed and watched as the men climbed aboard a pair of cars, fitting their large frames behind the wheels.

"Keep as far away from them as you can," said Tweed to his friend. "Try to avoid them so they can't get close enough to say . . . or *do* anything."

Just at that moment, the electricity was turned on, and the boys, after banging into a couple of six-year-old bumper motorists, took to the outside. As Tweed was about to manipu-

late his vehicle between two other cars, he and his car took a tremendous jolt from the rear. As he was spun around, he was struck again, first from Scarface on the left, followed by Slouch Hat on the right.

As Slouch Hat's vehicle struck Tweed's car a second time, the burly ruffian extended his left arm and squeezed the boy's shoulder. It hurt.

"You kids back off if you know what's good for you," bellowed Slouch Hat.

"And we want those pictures," yelled Scarface, just as his bumper careened into Tweed from the opposite side. "You two boys and us are going to go for a little walk when we get off this ride. We need to have a little talk. If you don't do what you're told, it might be curtains for you."

"Got that, kid?" said the other villain, his face twisted in rage.

Just then Doc came to Tweed's rescue by ramming his vehicle headlong into the bumper driven by Slouch Hat. Then he whirled and turned on Scarface. Tweed came alive and rammed one of the men from the other side. The jousting match continued until the power was turned off and the cars coasted to a stop. The boys had anticipated the end and already had their seat belts unbuckled. They jumped from their cars, careened out of the bumper car ride and raced through the Midway, bumping into other pedestrians one after another.

"Are they following?" yelled Doc, breathing hard. "They were a little slow getting out of their cars."

"Duck in here," said Tweed, pointing to the House of Mirrors. "They'll never find us in here even if they saw us going in."

But Tweed's assessment had maybe been a little off. The two men appeared just as the boys entered the mirrored maze. With their hands outstretched, the boys tiptoed forward through the catacomb of mirrors, which cast both plain and curved reflections. Tweed wondered briefly if the curved mirrors were concave or convex, but that wasn't as important as getting away from Slouch Hat and Scarface. They ran through the maze of mirrors, hardly noticing that their images shrank like mushrooms and grew tall and thin as they passed.

Their hands slid helplessly down each mirror, their feet seemingly stepping in every direction at once. Twice they tripped over each other, and more than once, bumped their shoulders and elbows on unyielding panels of glass. Tweed remembered suddenly that to find the way out one had to look at the floor to determine direction. He didn't want to have to explain all that, so he just whispered, "Follow me," and led the way down one of the passages.

Doc bumped his head against a wall of glass, and he lost sight of his companion. "Where are you, Tweed? I've lost you!" he said, panic rising to his throat.

"Over here. Keep moving forward."

Groping the mirrored surfaces with his hands, Doc found an opening and passed through it. As his shoulder rubbed polished glass to his right, he stepped forward through another passage and still another. Tweed's voice stayed directly in front of him:

"I'm waiting for you. Keep coming. I think you're on the right track."

Doc was making progress, but he had to be very careful of taking a wrong turn into one of the dead ends. The beckoning glass, containing all those images of himself, yawned before him and made every barrier appear as if it were a passageway. He asked himself if he had been in this spot before and began believing he was merely stumbling in circles.

Then his probing fingers touched the fabric of Tweed's shirt. "My gosh, I was so scared," stuttered Doc.

A cold, deep voice said, "Gottya!" and an iron grip closed around his wrist. "You've gone to the fair for the last time, kiddie."

Doc twisted and turned to no avail, but his teeth found the man's hand, and he bit him as hard as he could. The man yowled, and Doc broke free. Racing blindly through the mirrored tunnels, banging repeatedly against what seemed a prison of glass, he stumbled blindly through the maze. Another hand grasped his shoulder, and he started to scream, but a hand clamped over his mouth. His terrified gaze slid up to meet . . . the eyes of his friend Tweed.

He would have told Tweed how relieved he was to see him, but, between gasping for breath and being so scared, he didn't think the words would come out. Tweed had a firm hold of his arm and pulled Doc through the maze. "I think I've found the way out. Hold my hand," Tweed whispered and led the way.

Doc did as he was told. Soon the boys passed through a dark tunnel into a gauntlet of teetering barrels, floors that pushed up under their feet, and a hallway that greeted them with electric shocks every time they touched the wall. Then they stumbled onto the long, meandering slide that seemed to have no bottom but within moments deposited them outside in front of the House of Mirrors.

"We're free," shouted Doc. "I've never been so happy to see daylight before in my whole life. Scarface had me, and I bit him. I think he plans to kill us."

"Well, we're not free yet," warned Tweed. "Look over there in front of the ticket booth."

"Slouch Hat!" said Doc with a gulp.

The man started in their direction.

As the boys darted into the crowds, Tweed said between pants: "Only Scarface went in. Pretty smart! They left one guy

71

outside while the other went looking for us. But I think Slouch Hat'll have to wait for Scarface to find his way out of the maze. And that could take some doing."

They raced from the Midway and didn't stop until they reached the concessions area just across the street. They hoped they could locate a police officer, but there were so many people sauntering in every direction, they were lucky to find their way at all.

"I know Grandpa likes the Ye Olde Mill ride when he comes to the fair," ventured Tweed. "It is right up the street about another block. Maybe we can find him there. He loves that boat ride through the dark."

The aroma of foot-long hotdogs and Pronto Pups no longer tempted them as they made their way in the direction of the mill. The boys knew they had to put some space between them and their pursuers and hustled as fast as the crowds allowed.

"Scarface should be out by now," said Doc, glancing back at the sea of faces. "I sure hope Grandpa West is at the mill."

"If not, we're sure to find him somewhere on Machinery Hill," whispered Tweed, who continuously looked over his right shoulder.

They reached the mill, but in doing so, glimpsed the two thugs advancing up the middle of the street.

"What'll we do?" said Doc, trying to hide behind a sapling of an ash tree. "They'll see us any minute."

"No, they won't," said Tweed with determination, ducking into the rear of the line for the mill ride and pulling Doc with him. "They should walk right past us."

Luck, however, was not with them as the two men, looking up and down the street, moved in their direction. The line had progressed up to the ticket booth, and the boys hastily purchased ride tickets and tried to keep people between them and the men.

"I think they've spotted us again," whispered Doc. "They are getting in line."

"This guy in front of us is pretty big. If we need help, I bet he'd throttle those crooks to impress his girlfriend."

Several persons disembarked from the boats while others quickly took their places and disappeared into the darkness of the watery tunnel. Reaching the landing, the big man and his sweetheart climbed into the front seat of the just vacated boat. Tweed and Doc scampered behind them into the second row as a young lady and her little daughter were about to step down into the row behind them.

But Scarface and Slouch Hat were not about to let their quarry elude them again. Scarface jumped in front of the startled woman and squeezed her out of the way. Before either Tweed or Doc could emit a cry, the boat jerked forward with Scarface and Slouch Hat in the row behind them. Immediately each boy felt a snakelike arm coil around their throats and heard a raspy voice utter close to their ears, "Now we've got you." Then there was only darkness.

Chapter Seven

trapped!

From beside the splashing wheel the boat began its journey through what should have been a veritable dreamland. As the boys and their captors made their descent into the maelstrom, they could hear the thumping of the ride's forty-horsepower electric motor turning the huge paddlewheel to generate the current necessary to push the boats. But while other enthusiastic fair-goers teetered on their seats in the clattering catacomb, Tweed and Doc grappled with their more powerful adult adversaries. As they passed their first diorama, the big man and his sweetheart, seated in front of them, turned towards them in the semi-darkness. For a few seconds, the dark passage was illuminated by the somber red light of the icebergs and polar bears of the "Land of the Midnight Sun" scene. The couple in front stared at them.

"What's going on back there?" said the man, then his voice took on more dangerous tones. "What are you doing to those kids?" He started to clamber over the seat. "Maybe you should pick on someone your own size."

"They're runaways," said Scarface with a lot less confidence than just a moment before. "One of 'em's my son . . ."

Paying no attention and encouraged by his girlfriend, who was saying, "Oh, those poor little boys," the big man grabbed Scarface by the neck and shook him. Both boys broke free when Scarface was lifted roughly out of the boat and pitched into the water behind them. Before he broke the water's black surface, a huge right hand struck Slouch Hat's jaw, catapulting him into the water on top of his crony. As the boat progressed through the darkness, miserable shouts of, "Help, I'm drowning," and a great deal of splashing about were heard in the murky gloom. A loud thump convinced the boys that the boat coming up behind them had bumped into the two men thrashing about in the tunnel.

"We sure want to thank you for pummeling those crooks, mister," said Doc in a thin voice. "They've been following us all around town for days. I think they're trying to kidnap us. If it weren't for you . . . we'd be in deep water."

"Now *they* are," quipped Tweed, still watching fearfully behind the boat.

"My name's Clark Hansen," said the man, "and this is my fiancée Andrea Dawn."

Hansen had climbed back into his own seat and snugged an arm around the pretty woman, who looked up at him with adoring eyes that clearly said, "My hero."

Clark grinned proudly. "I manage a fitness club and occasionally get involved in a little commercial television. Here's my card. If those two goons ever bother you again, don't hesitate to call me. You both seem like nice young men. It really upsets me to see someone treat good boys like this." He looked at his girlfriend, who smiled with approval. "When we get to the dock, I want you boys to clear out of here. I'll deal with those two guys when they come out of the tunnel. Believe me, boys, they'll look like two drowned rats. I don't think they'll be in any shape to cause you any further trouble today. Do you want me to nab them and hold them for the police?"

"Naw!" replied Tweed with way more calm and bravery than Doc felt at the moment. "You see, sir . . . er . . . Clark, we're kind of junior detectives working on a case. We're very close to cracking it, and I think those two guys know it. But, gee, thanks again for rescuing us. We won't forget it."

The man gave them a dark look. "That doesn't seem like such a good idea, boys—"

But the boat had stopped at the landing, and the two boys jumped out and rushed into the crowd. Doc, looking over his shoulder, crashed into a man eating a funnel cake. Apologizing, he whispered to Tweed that he thought he had caught a glance of Mr. Hanson holding the two gruff-looking men by the collars back at the mill, but he couldn't be sure.

Then the boys met up with a little luck—they found Grandfather West in front of the Horticulture Building. After relating their latest encounter with the crooks, the trio walked to the car and drove home with the sun still high in the afternoon sky.

They spent the evening listening to their favorite rock groups on CDs and making plans for the next day. Grandfather West suggested they stay home and slow down a bit on cracking their case, but the boys begged him to drive them downtown St. Paul in the morning for some "safe" sleuthing. Tweed was convinced that there was no time to waste, that the two crooks would be moving on once they completed their illicit operation. He felt they might find some answers with another research trip to the library. There seemed to be an abundance of material on Pig's-Eye the smuggler but little on Fountain Cave itself.

Both boys, exhausted from their ordeal that day and the poor night's sleep the night before, fell asleep way earlier than either had planned and slept soundly through the night. There were no intruders to disturb their slumber. Mustard kept vigil at the bedroom window, and a patrol car cruised the neighborhood at close intervals.

The next morning dawned clear and blue, and even through the window, the sun felt hot.

Tweed pulled a blue "Save Our Wildlife" t-shirt over his head, ran a washcloth across his face, and motioned to Doc to follow him into the kitchen. Doc slipped his favorite Doc Savage novel, *The Thousand-Headed Man*, into the pouch pocket by the knee of his pants and groggily followed his friend into the kitchen.

While Doc slurped the milk from his cereal and wiped peanut butter from his mouth, Tweed searched the ground outside for possible footprints. He found nothing, not even raccoon tracks, to indicate that anyone or anything had approached the house while they slept. Satisfied, he went back inside and returned to his breakfast.

As he munched the last of his cereal, Grandfather West's bedroom door opened, and the older man joined them at the table.

"I'll drive you into the loop," he told the boys, "and then I have to get back here to meet Cranky Edwards for some fishing. I'm trusting that you two will go to the nearest cop if there's the slightest indication of trouble." He eyed them critically. "And if you even catch sight of those two men, you call the cops straight away. Right?"

Both boys nodded vigorously.

Mr. Edwards, who's real first name was Crandall, although everyone called him Cranky because he frequently complained about wearing tight shoes, was an old family friend. Grandfather West told them what a good fisherman Cranky was but said he would deny having paid his friend a compliment if the boys related that to the old gentleman.

"And let's be clear on this last thing," said Grandfather West softly, as if someone was listening. "You boys are going to spend the day at the *library*. Nowhere else. Don't wander about town. And absolutely stay away from that cave. About five, you're going to call me, then take a bus to Doc's sister's,where you'll spend the night. Remember to call me when you get to Elizabeth's and Andy's so I know you're okay. Promise?"

Both boys agreed. Within minutes they were riding in Grandfather's pickup down West Seventh Street past the old Czech Hall where Czechs, Slovaks, and Moravians congregated. At Seven Corners, they turned down Fifth Street where Grandfather West left the boys in front of the Landmark Center, which had served as the Federal Courts Building for half a century.

"There's a courtroom in there that was the site of many infamous gangster trials during the 1930s," announced Tweed. "Some of the FBI's most notorious criminals were tried in the building, including: Ma Barker and her five sons, Alvin 'Creepy' Karpis, Baby Face Nelson, John Dillinger, and his gal Evelyn Freschette, and even Machine Gun Kelly. FBI G-men, armed with Thompson sub-machine guns, kept guard in the upper balconies to ward off any courtroom escape attempts or ambushes."

Doc wondered if they were dealing with modern gangsters, but he didn't mention this as they turned into Rice Park, flanked by the Ordway Center for the Performing Arts on one side and the St. Paul Hotel on the other.

"Once," said Tweed, "they had statues here in the park of Charlie Brown and Snoopy."

When they were dropped off, the boys scampered up the stairs and entered the library, heading directly to the reading room. Fifteen minutes later, they were once more poring over volumes of St. Paul history for information on the smuggler Pig's-Eye Parrant and his cave.

"Says here," whispered Tweed, "that old Pig's-Eye, 'a shady character with a bad reputation,' built a cabin at the mouth of the cave in 1838. He was described as 'a coarse, ill-looking, low-browed fellow, with only one serviceable eye.' The other was blind, sinister-looking, marble-hued and crooked, with a white ring glaring around the pupil. Two years later, the soldiers at Fort Snelling kicked him out. After that, the cave was used as a storehouse, then as a tourist attraction from 1850 to 1880. St. Paul residents visited the cave for its cool air and cooler water. In 1852 a pavilion was opened nearby, which offered refreshments and lights for exploring. Fountain Cave was even featured in the *Tourists' Guide to the Health and Pleasure Resorts of the Golden Northwest*. In the late 1800s, sewage and storm water were discharged through the cave by a railroad company. The cave wasn't so good as a tourist attraction after that. Development also damaged the area by filling the wetlands and slowing the flow of Fountain Creek into the cave. In 1960 the cave's entrance was buried during the construction of Shepard Road.

"But we already know all this about Pig's-Eye," said Doc. "What does it say about the *cave?*"

"I'm getting there," replied Tweed, who occasionally liked to keep his enthusiastic friend waiting and wondering. He lifted his eyes over the top of the book he was holding in front of him, then lowered them to read, "Fountain Cave was known as IN-YAN TI-PI by the local Dakota people. It was estimated to have been 1,150 feet in length, and was possibly Minnesota's longest natural sandstone cave. The formation of the cave was a result of erosion. As stream water made its way to the Mississippi, the sandstone wore away.'" Tweed lifted his eyes again. "In the old days, the cave was called 'one of the greatest curiosities and wonders of the West,' and tourists came here from all over the country. They used to conduct guided tours and rent lamps to visitors, even sold ice cream. Inside the cave, a 150-foot-long winding hall led to a beautiful circular room about fifty feet in diameter."

"That's it!" shouted Doc carelessly, causing everyone in the room to look up from their books and frown at him. "Somewhere in that large circular room is where they keep all the stuff they're smuggling. It's gotta be!"

"I agree," whispered Tweed, "but that cave's been blown apart for years. Heck, we tried to find an entrance, and you saw how far we got."

"But we *did* see those two galoots step out of those rocks," said Doc. "And those kids went somewhere—" He paused when he saw Tweed face go white.

"Don't look now," Tweed said, "but I think I just saw a familiar face behind that newspaper two rows over."

Doc gulped. "You mean . . . you mean they're even in *here* watching us?"

"I don't know," said Tweed in the crowded reading room. "Let's find out."

Doc felt his heart thump. "What do you have in mind?"

Tweed shrugged. "Well, think about it. We're pretty safe in here. You walk around his table on the left, and I'll come around from the right. If it is not Slouch Hat or Scarface, we'll just keep walking."

"But, what if . . . ?"

"If it is one of them, I'll whap him over the head with this heavy history book. You scream for the librarian. The cops'll come and lock him up."

Doc said nothing but slowly rose from his chair and sauntered as casually as his knocking knees could manage along the row in the direction of the man with the hidden face while Tweed crept around the other side. As they approached their quarry, they found themselves in a quandary. The man turned a page of his paper and Doc thought he saw a scar on the man's left cheek, but he wasn't sure. Truthfully, the man had his face buried in his newspaper. Doc could see clearly only the back of his head.

Doc's nerves had him shaking, his heart thumping. Suddenly, he couldn't stand the suspense. He shouted so loud everyone in the room jumped. "It's him, Tweed! It's him! Bash him!"

Tweed walloped the man over the head with the oversized, heavy book. The man lurched, the newspaper fell, and everyone in the room gasped. Tweed, the book still in his hands, stared at the man he had hit. Slowly, the man regained his posture, set his glasses back on his nose and turned around to face his attackers. He narrowed his eyes, all the while hissing like a dangerous snake. Both boys recoiled, their faces blossoming red with embarrassment. They had struck an innocent man, and he bolted to his feet and reached for them.

"Look, sir," cried Tweed, dropping the book and backing away. "We apologize! We thought you were someone else. My friend here screamed and I . . . well . . . I just overreacted. We'll be glad to pay for any damages."

"Get out of my sight!" roared the man. "If I ever see you in here again, I'll call both your parents *and* the police."

"Yessir. We're really very sorry, sir," said Tweed. The boys backed a few more steps, apologizing to the librarians as well. When they reached the door, they turned and fled. Once in the hallway, they ran full tilt for the exit, galloped across Rice Park and did not stop until they reached the large parking lot on Fifth Street. Here they collapsed, gasping for breath.

"Boy, you sure got us in hot water," said Tweed.

Doc gave him a hopeless look. "I saw a scar. I saw a scar and panicked." He hung his head. "Now we can't even go into the library again."

Tweed patted his friend's shoulder. "Aw, we'll be able to go back, but not for a week or so."

The boys began walking west on Seventh Street. After a few blocks, they paused and scanned in all directions for signs of anyone following them. They saw no one, not the two thugs nor the angry man they had smacked with a book in the library. They realized that, for the first time in days, no one was on their tails.

"Come on," said Tweed. "Let's go look one more time for the entrance to Pig's-Eye Cave. I want to see that big room, and this time no one's going to stop us because no one knows we're here."

They proceeded cautiously along the river. Tweed pointed out the High Bridge. "That's the new bridge," he told Doc. "The old bridge was torn down in 1988. That one was built in the 1880s for horses, wagons, and carriages. Ahead, not far from the cave, is the old Northern States Power Company Plant that used to produce electricity for five hundred thousand homes. Across the river in those bluffs were the mushroom caves where they used to grow mushrooms for at least a century. Up river is the old swing-bridge built in 1915."

Doc smirked at Tweed. "Somehow I just knew I was going to get another history lesson," but Tweed knew he was just teasing, maybe even trying to distract him from worrying.

They arrived at the Pig's-Eye cave parking lot, which was empty of cars and people, and slipped into the thickets that reached up from the ravine.

"Follow me," whispered Tweed, who started to climb carefully down the riverbank. Doc, uneasy both because they were so close to where the horrid men might be and because there was almost no room to put his feet, took extra care. Flopping into the dirty river was not his idea of a good time.

Just ahead of him, Tweed pointed. "See the orange posts ahead of us? The ravine doubles back toward the highway. The cave is at the head of the ravine." He paused and crouched, Doc matching him. Tweed looked at him and said, "Okay, now think about this. In the 1830s, the cave had a stream of water coming out of its mouth. All the early explorers stopped to fill their canteens in that fresh, artesian spring. If we do find the entrance to the cave, I have a feeling we're going to get our feet wet."

Doc figured that was probably true. They continued up the ravine. Stumbling, almost crawling, the two boys jumped at the crashing sound of barges being loaded at the nearby grain elevators. They met each other's startled eyes and sighed. Slowly they made their way up the steep embankment and took cover behind a huge rock. They sat for what seemed like hours before Doc scrambled up the cliff to see if any cars were parked on the lot above the cave. Discovering that the lot was still empty, he slid back down and conveyed the news to Tweed.

"I don't think anyone's here right now. Ready to look for that secret entrance again?"

"Remember that broken branch on the tree over there? When we spotted those two baboons from the balloon, weren't they somewhere behind it a few feet?"

Doc looked. "You're right. But are you sure that's the same tree?"

"Pretty sure," replied Tweed, moving cautiously toward the broken branch. Doc hurried after him, staying only a step or two behind. "There's got to be a secret entrance in that rock face somewhere."

"But we already checked this out and found nothing but mosquitoes."

Tweed turned and met Doc's eyes. "Then we missed something. That guy's head came out of somewhere, and those kids went somewhere."

Despite a two-hour search, the boys turned up nothing. They were about to give up when Doc pointed at the broken tree branch and the debris-filled thicket beneath it.

"Of course," whispered Tweed triumphantly. "Doc, I think you did it!"

Crawling under the branch, the boys sifted through the debris and pushed aside the bushes with their arms. On the rough path in front of them was a weed-encrusted board half-standing in the foliage. Both boys lifted the board away from the side of the hill. Suddenly they were staring into a dark, damp, dreary tunnel that could only be the entrance to Pig's-Eye Cave.

"We found it!" crowed Doc, just a little too loudly under the circumstances.

"Shut up!" said Tweed quickly, "or they'll find us!"

Stepping into the dark tunnel, Doc produced a small flashlight from his knee pocket. "And you thought I just kept my Doc Savage novel in there, didn't you?" he said when Tweed stared in wonderment.

"Doc, I could hug you. Well, at least shake your hand," Tweed said, clapping his friend's shoulder.

The two boys eased cautiously through the long, narrow, winding passageway, plugging their noses from the stench of sewage-laced mud that soon covered their shoes. They had not expected the sharp drop in temperature on such a hot summer day, but just a few feet in from the entrance the tunnel felt positively chilly. The beam of the flashlight created eerie shadows on the walls, and Doc nearly choked when he thought he saw a bat hovering near the ceiling. A close inspection, however, revealed only a flitting shadow caused by their movement behind the steady glow of orange light.

The tunnel floor became wetter, until they were actually walking in water that rose to about the height of their shoes. "I hope it's not too much farther," said Doc. "I don't like it here."

"We should be entering that large, circular room soon. I only hope the water doesn't get any deeper in the meanwhile."

At the far end of the tunnel, they crawled through a tight passageway. Sooner than expected, the boys came upon a large, circular room, about fifty feet in diameter. As Doc illuminated the center of the chamber with his flashlight beam, both boys gulped simultaneously.

"Oh, my gosh!" croaked Doc, directing his light clockwise through the room. There must be 200 bicycles in here!"

"At least," said Tweed. "And every one of them brand new or almost new. All are very expensive bikes, too."

"Those kids we saw riding those bikes in here. They were stealing 'em, I bet, for Slouch Hat and Scarface. This is some kind of thief ring, Tweed. It's like the ghost of Pig's-Eye Parrant is still haunting this cave!"

"Thieves, maybe, but no ghosts. I think we know what those two are up to now. Let's get out of here, and go to the police so they can nab them."

As they turned to retrace their steps, they froze when they heard first splashing followed by soft voices.

The boys crouched. Doc felt that oh, so familiar panic push into him. "It's them—Slouch Hat and Scarface," he hissed to Tweed. "They're here, and they going to kill us. We didn't cover up the entrance behind us. It's curtains for us!"

Tweed pressed his palm over Doc's mouth. In a low voice right in his ear, he said, "Quick! Douse your light. Take my hand. Let's move deeper into the cave. Perhaps we can find a hiding place somewhere, maybe another exit."

But they had taken only a few steps when Slouch Hat and Scarface, both carrying flashlights, entered the room. The boys ducked behind a rock to avoid being detected, although they knew sanctuary was only temporary and not very good. The bright, spectral beam of the men's flashlights produced a bigger-than-life-sized shadow of Slouch Hat on the wall opposite them. Both boys held their breaths, afraid to breathe.

Then Scarface's voice boomed through the cavern as if electronically amplified: "You boys have caused your last bit of trouble. You'll never leave this cave alive!"

Chapter Eight

missing chums

Elizabeth Decker picked up the telephone on the third ring after wiping her hands on her apron, for she often baked cookies in the evening. She immediately recognized the voice of Tweed Salter's grandfather, Joe West.

"Are the boys there, Beth?" he asked. "Tweed told me he'd call about five when they left the library. Here it's seven o'clock. Are they there? I swear that boy can't remember anything from one minute to the next."

"They're coming here tonight?" she inquired with a touch of concern. "Joe, I haven't heard from Doc or Tweed all day."

"They were planning to spend the night at your place. Tweed promised me he'd call."

"Yes, when I talked with Doc yesterday, he said they might spend tonight here, but I haven't heard from them all day. I figured they weren't coming. Where do you think they are?"

"I dropped them off downtown to do some more research at the library on Pig's-Eye Cave. They were going to spend the day there and then call when they were ready to get on the bus to your place. They should have been perfectly safe. But, they haven't called, and the library's closed."

"You don't suppose they'd be foolish enough to go tramping around that cave after all that's happened, do you?"

"Maybe we had better call the police," said Joe West.

Elizabeth's voice sounded shaky when she said, "I'll tell Andy to call them. One of us will call you back in a few minutes. Please stay by your phone."

"Okay. Please hurry!"

After filling her husband Andy in on what was transpiring, Elizabeth Decker dialed the police and handed the receiver to Andy. She often became slightly incoherent during an apparent emergency, while Andy usually stayed pretty calm. That wasn't to say that Andy Decker couldn't get tough on occasion. He'd proven that at the polo match. As a younger man, he had won the St. Paul East Side Middleweight Boxing title by knocking out an opponent at least a head taller than he.

Andy asked for Sergeants Berven or Riley but neither officer was on duty that evening. The officer on the phone felt there was a good chance that the boys would soon show up— "They usually do," quipped the officer—but a patrol car was sent to pick up photos of the boys just in case they didn't. Officers were sent to the library and also to Fountain Cave. Andy gave the officer his cell phone number and asked him to pass it along to Sergeant Berven in the morning. Andy thanked him and hung up.

"Beth, call Mr. West back. Tell him what the officer said," Andy said. "I'm going to grab Wally. We'll take a drive and see if we can find the boys. Call me on my cell if you hear anything."

Elizabeth looked fearful. "Oh, Andy, you aren't going to that awful cave in the dark, are you? You could lose your footing and slip into the river or break a leg climbing about those rocks. Besides, who knows who or what's lurking in that spooky cave."

"The cave's all sealed up. I doubt anyone'll be there. And the police are going to be there anyway. I promise to play it safe and take no unnecessary chances. Wally and I'll merely take a look around. We may not even go to the cave. Hopefully, the boys will show up here in a little while with some story to tell, and we won't have to do much snooping around at all."

Andy kissed Elizabeth lightly on the cheek and picked up his friend and neighbor Wally Baard. Within minutes the pair rode slowly in Andy's pickup along Payne Avenue on St. Paul's East Side. Andy pulled over on a little side street, offset on a corner lot, and pointed towards a tunnel leading from the city above into a large ravine below.

"Doc and Tweed often played here other summers," said Andy. "Of course, I don't think they'd be down there this late, but who knows. As Tweed Salter would tell you straight from his encyclopedic brain, this was the only road in or out of that hidden valley called 'Swede Hollow,' where one of Minnesota's oldest and most overlooked immigrant settlements flourished for 140 years. The Hollow was named by its earliest arrivals, Swedish peasants, who called it Svenska Dalen, or 'Swedish Dale,' and for over a century it was a haven for wave after wave of poor immigrant families. Tweed's obsessed with the history of this sort. I doubt it, but they could be down there."

The two men climbed from the pickup, each equipped with a flashlight, slipped through the tunnel, and started down the hill to another world.

"They could be hiking along Phalen Creek down there, I suppose," stammered Wally in an uneasy tone. "They're so drawn to local history, and the park's so close to your house, they could be down there. I think I read somewhere that the shanties once nestled down here were quite a contrast to the elegant Victorian mansions directly above on Dayton's Bluff."

"Tweed, with Doc's help, once wrote an article on it and submitted it to a magazine. Although it wasn't published, the editor wrote back that he was really impressed with Tweed's knowledge of historic St. Paul."

"Well, there's Phalen Creek, pretty much still flowing the length of the valley. If the boys are here, I'd think they'd be by the creek or what's left of it. It's pretty dry."

Andy remembered that the creek was named for the first white inhabitant, Edward Phalen. Tweed had been especially interested in this because there was a bit of a mystery attached to it. Edward Phalen later murdered a man, and the creek was the only one in America to be named after a murderer. With that thought in his head, Andy's concern rose.

After canvassing the valley with their flashlights and calling out for the boys' several times, Andy and Wally were satisfied that the boys were not in the park. Deciding to take a quick drive through downtown St. Paul—mainly checking out bus stops where the boys generally waited—they started back up the hill towards the lights of Payne Avenue.

Darkness was now pretty much complete, and both men kept an eye on their feet to avoid a fall. A light wind whistled across the valley below them, and once Andy thought he heard the frightened voice of Tweed calling out from the void. But it was only the wind, and neither man believed in ghosts.

"Boy, that sure is a spooky place once it gets dark," said Wally, more than once looking over his shoulder toward what he imagined as spectral footsteps.

Okay so Andy wasn't so sure what Wally believed regarding ghosts. "Yeah," he said almost defiantly. "But think about what it was like when those poor folks lived in those decrepit, rotting old shanties. It was even more what we'd call another world then. As the city grew, life for the residents of Swede Hollow remained primitive. Fresh springs provided their only drinking water, and electricity was unattainable. In fact, the creek served as their sewer as well as their water supply. Newly arrived immigrants walked up the railway tracks from Union Depot, directed to relatives' homes by notes pinned to their lapels. Many simply moved into the first vacant house they reached. Tweed told me lots more about the hollow." Andy realized that the only reason he was prattling on about Swede Hollow was to keep his head on straight. It was working only so far. He was really starting to worry about the boys.

A quick drive through the loop turned up nothing, and Andy's anxiety began to heighten. Wally was sympathetic and attempted in to keep conversation going, but Andy had become grimly silent. He was worried. The man he had confronted after the polo match certainly had been persistent enough following them to have spotted the boys after that.

After a final check of all the bus stops along Seventh Street, Andy stopped for the red light at St. Peter Street and looked at his friend. Wally knew what was coming.

"I'm going to head out to the cave," Andy said as if convincing himself of what he must do. "It's the only place they could be. Something's wrong, and it has something to do with that cave. I just know it. It's going to be dangerous stumbling along those rocky cliffs with the river right below, so if you want to wait in the truck, I'll understand."

"Hey, amigo," replied Wally. "I signed on to find the boys with you. I'm not quitting until we either locate them or you decide to go home."

Andy turned left off Kellogg Boulevard and drove slowly down the steep hill to Shepard Road and the river. The lights of metro St. Paul flickered in his rear view mirror as he descended the hill, and the aroma of fine foods being prepared in the Italian and Irish restaurants above them filling their nostrils.

"You're a true friend, Wally, and I appreciate it," Andy murmured to Wally. "Besides, I might need your fists before this night is over, and you always did have a pretty good right."

There was little traffic on Shepard Road, and the dim lighting only increased the festering gloom that hung over them. Once a boat on the river to their left tooted its deep nasal horn, and the beam from its light created grotesque dancing shadows on the murky river. There was something macabre about the night, but both men were determined to find the boys no matter what.

As they approached the small Fountain Cave parking lot and historical marker, Wally was surprised when Andy continued past the site.

"I know," said Andy, "you're wondering why I didn't pull in back there. The main cave is under the roadway there, but that doesn't mean the entrance is there as well. I'm sure we aren't going to see anything in the dark, but Pig's-Eye Cave was part of a huge labyrinth running under this whole part of the city. The labyrinth connected several important caves in addition to Pig's-Eye. The Marina Caves, Banholzer Cave, Stahlmann's Cellars, and an eerie one called Smuggler's Cave. There were also several unnamed ones, some natural, some not, that could be accessed by way of the labyrinth. I'm hoping something'll catch my eye, and we can find a doorway of sorts to that labyrinth."

Andy drove along Shepard Road past the old Northern States Power facility, slowed up to take a good look at the river bank, pulled into a driveway and turned the truck around so it faced the river. He stopped for what seemed to Wally several minutes, shining his high beams on the bank. He then veered right again up a hill toward West Seventh. Here, the road turned abruptly left where it met up with Randolph.

Continuing south along the river, they passed a small brick building on their right, which appeared to be a small construction yard. On one side of the building, they saw the sealed off old entrance to the Schmitt Caves, the sign faded and peeling.

"I think we can slip into that tunnel here," said Andy. "The edge of that concrete slab has been worn away or chopped through by kids. I don't think this'll take us in Pig's-Eye, though, because this entrance was the main way into the portion that was machine cut into the sandstone and limestone. They probably dead-ended it pretty quick when they closed the caves.

Andy slipped through the aperture easily enough, although Wally, slightly plump, had a tougher time of it. Once inside, the two men turned on their flashlights and surveyed the arched ceiling and rough, flat walls. Old gas lamp pipes, nearly hidden by festoons of spider webs jutted from the walls as the pair progressed into the unknown.

"I don't think the boys got in this way," said Wally, as they entered the main chamber. "Outside of bats and spiders, and perhaps a few curious kids, I don't think anyone has been in here in a long time."

"You just said the magic words, though, Wally," whispered Andy. "'A few curious kids.' We're looking for two of 'em."

The passage led to more rooms, shaped almost like a ladder with rungs forty feet long. Moving steadily along, they eventually entered older, more natural parts of the caves. They passed through a series of meandering rooms and passages, which covered a subterranean area a quarter mile on each side. One passage led them out to the hillside above the river on the opposite side of the road from the construction company yard. It was apparent to both men that much of the cave laid beneath Shepard Road and the older homes in the neighborhood.

Before stepping out onto the river bank, Wally peered through a jagged hole in a wall and saw what was once an old spring running through the cavern at one end. Andy climbed through the archway into the spring-bed and found the bottom paved with rows of old red bricks, which extended up the walls a few feet.

He said to Wally: "I think this is an old storm sewer. I'm pretty sure we're in a corner of old Pig's-Eye Cave, but I don't see any way of going farther underground. Let's head back to the truck and take a look at where the cave marker stands adjacent to that little turn-off. On the way, I'll call Beth on my cell and see if there's anything new on that end."

The two men walked along the river towards the pickup. Crickets chirped sharply from the thicket on their left and an occasional motorist drove by on Shepard Road. Reaching the truck, they climbed in and started back toward Pig's Eye Cave.

"Don't look now," said Andy with an eye on his rear view mirror, "but maybe we're being followed. That green car behind us is the same car, I think, that drove past us while we were walking back to the truck. Get ready, Wally, there may be a little action slated for us. I've tangled with these guys already, and they don't mind mixing it up."

The green vehicle maintained a comfortable distance behind them, and the beam from the headlights cast an eerie glow on their rear window. Andy wanted desperately to pull over, but there was no place to do so. He cleared his throat, winked at Wally, and said, "In a minute or two we'll be pulling into the cave lot. Then we'll see what those birds are up to."

"Slow down a little and see what they do," said Wally.

Andy decreased his speed to fifteen miles per hour. The green car, however, just slowed down and kept pace.

"I'd think he'd have attempted to pass us if he wasn't up to anything," said Wally, glancing into the passenger-side mirror.

"We'll find out right now," said Andy, as he steered the car into the parking lot of Pig's-Eye Cave and shut down the engine.

The green car also pulled in and parked on the other end of the lot. Andy and Wally remained in their vehicle, allowing whoever was in the other vehicle to make the next move. No one, however, stepped out of the green car. With its tinted windows hiding who was inside, it was impossible for Andy and Wally to see even how many persons were in the car.

"They're watching us. I can feel it," whispered Wally. "I think they want us to make the first move. Who knows what's waiting for us in that car."

For ten minutes, nothing happened to end the stalemate. No one from either vehicle stepped out into the dreary lot. It was almost as if the occupants of both were afraid of the other. Finally, Andy poked Wally's arm and said, "This is abominable. Waiting is getting us nowhere. Let's do it!"

Both men stepped from the pickup and began walking in the direction of the green car. Suddenly both doors opened, but for a second or two no one climbed out. Wally and Andy paused, not knowing what to make of the situation. As they started forward again, a young man stepped out on the driver's side and a pretty, young lady from the passenger side.

Then, as if for the first time, the young man saw Andy and Wally approaching. He paused, almost pulled back into his car, then said, "Um . . . can I help you?" He sounded a little frightened.

The young lady came around the car, grabbed the young man's hand, and pulled him away. "Tommy, I told you not to stop here!" In a moment, they had disappeared, running down the blacktopped river walk parallel to Shepard Road.

"Jiminy," whispered Wally. "Just a couple kids wanting to be alone, and we scared the heck out of them."

Kicking a little loose gravel, Andy breathed a sign of relief, looked up sheepishly and replied, "And I hate to admit it, but I think they scared the heck out off us, too."

Walking to the edge of the rocky hill, the two men turned on their flashlights and began descending the incline.

"Be careful," said Andy. "It is pretty treacherous here in the dark, and it wouldn't take much to slip on one of these rocks to end us up in trouble."

"Any sign that the boys've been here?" asked Wally.

"I can't see well enough."

"I don't see any cave entrance. I can't see much of anything down there. I swear these mosquitoes are the size of bats . . . Bats? Do you think . . . ?"

"Shhh," whispered Andy, flicking off his flashlight and motioning for Wally to do the same. "Somebody's down here. I thought I heard a twig snap, and I definitely heard a low voice coming from those bushes."

Darkness filled in around them. "Maybe it's just that young couple we saw on the lot," whispered Wally.

"They're up above us, probably a mile from here. Stay down. Don't turn on your light. I think they might have seen the beams of our flashlights. Listen? Do you hear it? Sounds just like those voices are coming right out of those rocks."

"I'm going down there," said Wally with sudden conviction. "If these are the bums that've been giving the kids trouble, they're going to wish they never tangled with *me*. Cover me, Andy. I'm going down into those bushes."

"Cover you with what? My cane?" said Andy. "We'll go together. There's more than one person down there. People don't usually talk out loud to themselves. And who knows what they're carrying. Careful now. Follow me and slide on your rump."

As they maneuvered toward the clump of bushes, they no longer heard voices. They expected to be hit over the head at any second by some unseen marauder waiting in ambush. Reaching the thicket, however, they found no one, although the bushes appeared to have recently been disturbed.

"Somewhere here is the entrance to that cave," concluded Andy in hushed tones. "It's got to be here somewhere, and I'm not leaving until we find it. I'm convinced the boys are somewhere in that cave, and I don't believe it's Pig's-Eye's ghost who's keeping them company."

"Couldn't those voices have been from someone walking the river trail?"

"There's no river trail down there. Too steep. If we go down any further, we'll end up in the Muddy Mississippi over our heads. Let's hide in these bushes and pray the mosquitoes don't make us go crazy."

Wally stumbled but recovered himself quickly. Without warning, he turned on his flashlight, pointing it at the ground. An angry Andy snapped in a low, harsh tone, "I told you not to turn that thing on."

Wally stooped and picked up something, which he showed to Andy. "Look," he said. "It was sticking out of those weeds."

Andy looked, seeing that Wally held a paperback book. He took it and scanned the cover. Just enough light came down from Shepard Avenue to illuminate the title. "It's one of those Doc Savage novels that Doc always carries in his pockets."

"Is it his?"

"I'm sure of it. Now we know the boys have been here and are probably in serious trouble!"

Chapter Nine

the ghost of pig's-eye parrant

Slouch Hat and Scarface stood menacingly in front of the rock that sheltered Tweed and Doc. Scarface attempted to shine his light behind the rock, but from where he was standing, he could see no trace of the boys. Doc felt a tickle in his throat and almost coughed, but by placing his hand over his nose and mouth, he suppressed the urge. The two villains walked slowly away from the rock and commenced lighting lanterns, four of them, that illuminated the interior of the chamber.

"That was a close one," whispered a shaking Tweed Salter. "Had you coughed, it would have been curtains for us. While they're busy lighting those lanterns, let's see if we can get deeper into the cave. Those bicycles should provide us with a little cover if we keep quiet." For a moment, he hesitated, watching the men. Then his husked, "Okay, follow me and walk on your toes."

Keeping low to the ground, the boys crept nearly on their knees beneath the flickering lantern light. Scarface had walked over to the tunnel entrance as if he had forgotten something of importance. Slouch Hat sat lazily on a rock ledge, scanning the chamber for his prey. Although he glanced in the boys' directions several times, he could see nothing but bicycles in the shadows.

The boys made their way past the bicycles, which represented a wide variety of styles and models, but most were expensive and all new or nearly so. Other than that, there seemed to be no rhyme or reason to the manner in which the stolen bicycles were stockpiled. The boys crawled quietly through a maze of racing bikes, touring bikes, hacked together ten speeds, and cross bikes.

Tweed began to understand. Each one of the bikes had special features, so if the crooks planned to sell them, there was certainly something there for everyone's taste. He even passed a mountain bike he had drooled over for months but knew he'd never afford. It'd sure be nice for short rides in heavy traffic, when the wind was not too strong.

They reached another huge boulder and slipped behind it to rest.

"Gosh," whispered Doc, "those touring bikes start at about $600 and go to over $2,100. I know because just a couple weeks ago my dad and I looked at some in Chicago."

Tweed shushed him, but he said very softly, "These guys are professional thieves. They only steal top-of-the-line stuff. Look at all those custom jobs. They're built one at a time—custom—with the lightest weight possible for someone's size and the way they're going to be ridden. We have to get out of here and tell the police."

"Do you think they really know we're in here? Maybe they're only bluffing."

Tweed didn't know. "They know someone discovered the entrance to this place. They know we're either hiding from them in here, or, hopefully, they think we dashed to the police, and they have to split pronto. If they do, we're out of here."

Standing erect, the boys slipped against the limestone walls and sidestepped deeper into the cave. Although it was dark, their fingers slid across the sides of the passage, and the flickering lanterns from across the chamber convinced Tweed that the walls were covered with Indian hieroglyphics representing birds, fish, and animals.

"I hate to tell you this now," said Tweed, inching along the rough wall, "but for several years, many of the Indians who remained here after the smuggler Parrant was banished, refused to enter the cave, believing that the 'Ghost of Pig's-Eye Parrant' still lingered inside."

"I don't believe in ghosts," Doc said, but his voice quavered.

"Me neither," said Tweed, "but it sure is spooky in here."

Out of the large room, they could see nothing and had to be careful not to step into a hole, stumble, or make any noise.

Doc husked, "What's that buzzing sound? It's like a bee hive close by in this same passage. Possible?"

"I don't think so," said Tweed, but he also heard the strange buzzing. "Maybe you better watch where you lay your hands, anyway."

After rounding a bend in the corridor, they crossed what felt like a narrow, sandstone tunnel. Doc bravely crawled a short distance into the tunnel, and returning to the main passage, indicated that it had collapsed and was closed with a recent rock fall.

Moving deeper along the open passage, Tweed teetered briefly and grabbed Doc's arm.

"Careful, Doc. There's some kind of pit here. I nearly fell into it. I think we can go around it, though."

For just a split second, Doc turned on his flashlight, illuminating the treacherous abyss that yawned in front of them. "Looks like it only drops about twenty feet or so," he ventured out loud. "But, if you had fallen in, you'd never get out without help. Besides, looks like a great place to break a leg. Here, take my wrist. Let's go around it."

As they sidestepped the precipice, they felt a flapping of wings soar over their heads.

"Oh, my, gosh!" cried Doc, a little too loudly. "A bat!"

"Or maybe just a lost bird," Tweed muttered. "Keep your voice down or the two 'birds' back there'll hear us."

Clasping hands, so as not to lose each other, they continued their trek through the cold, damp blackness until it became apparent that the space was physically too small for them to get through. It appeared to the boys that after the narrowest point, which a smaller person might have been able to wiggle through, the passage widened, but, with brief flicks of their light, they saw evidence of a recent rock fall in the back of the tunnel, and they couldn't pass.

Although each time they used the flashlight had risks, Tweed switched it on for a few seconds. The walls of the tunnel were much darker than those in the main chamber and were sooted. The ceiling looked almost red in color. Tweed pointed out that fire often turned sandstone red.

"There could be some vertical groove petroglyphs in here," whispered Tweed.

"Petro-what?" asked a bewildered Doc.

"Carvings or inscriptions on rocks made by Native Americans. The reference to the Parrant ghost could be a

Christianized translation of a Native American belief that a dangerous or evil spirit resided here. Ritual grooving would make sense if a dangerous spirit or 'devil' was believed to exist here. Powerful spirits related to illness were believed by the Ojibwa and other Algonquin peoples to live underground in the rock. The Ojibwa in northern Minnesota made sacrifices to it. Shamans believed they could enter the rock during altered states of consciousness and talk to the 'rock people' about how to treat the sick."

Doc shook his friend's arm and switched off the light. "Rock People! Spirits! What does all that have to do with the Pig's-Eye Ghost? Or, right now, with those two guys—?"

"The red stone in the back of the cave may have led them to believe a ghost resided here. Then when the settlers in this area heard those stories, they took for granted that it was Pig's-Eye Parrant's ghost that lingered. There were supposed to have been sightings of a ghost with a patch over his eye— Pierre Parrant!"

Doc grew frustrated. He shook Tweed again. "This is all very interesting, Professor Salter, but aren't you forgetting we're trapped in a haunted cave with two very real maniacs?"

Tweed pulled him down into a crouch. "Listen!" he said. "I hear footsteps . . . those loose stones back in the passageway. Did you just see a light flicker at the far side of the tunnel? It's Scarface and Slouch Hat, I just know it. They're coming for us. Our only hope is to try and make it back to that little side tunnel and see if we can't squeeze in."

"We'll never make it," Doc husked. "They're probably checking it out right now. Maybe we could . . . wallop them with a rock just as they reach us. We're hidden here. Maybe they'd walk past, and we could clock them good, then race back to the entrance in the confusion."

Tweed looked at the smaller boy, thinking.

103

"It's worth a try, isn't it?" Doc said.

"Those guys are pretty big and awfully mean. I don't know if it'll work, Doc."

"We can't wait here like trapped rats. Let's slide along the wall with those petro-whatevers. Who knows? Maybe we can sneak right past them. Let's go!"

The boys moved cautiously along the wall, attempting to backtrack in the darkness. As they progressed, the footsteps of the men grew louder. They were getting close. Occasionally the flickering of a flashlight ricocheted off the walls ahead of them, and both boys knew that within another minute or two, they'd come face to face with the two terrible men. Escape was next to impossible, but they were determined to go down fighting.

Rounding the curve in the passageway, the lights of their pursuers illuminated the tunnel. Doc poked Tweed in the side, certain they were seen. Tweed pointed to the little dead-end side tunnel, but with the thugs coming down on them, it was too late to duck into it.

"There they are!" shouted one of the villains, his deep voice reverberating through the gloom. "We've got 'em now. Don't try to run, boys, or it'll just go harder on you."

Suddenly, a loud, terrifying voice echoed out of nowhere: "Who dares disturb the sleep of Pig's-Eye Parrant?"

The voice boomed down the hall, causing the boys and their pursuers alike to stop and stand perfectly still.

"It's the ghost of Pig's-Eye Parrant!" There was no mistaking the horrified voice of Slouch Hat. "Quick! Douse your light! Maybe it can't see us in the dark."

"Yes, I am the spirit of Pig's-Eye Parrant. I allow no one to enter my realm in search of treasure," bellowed the voice of the invisible long-dead smuggler. "Go, or you shall all die! GO NOW!" Then the disembodied voice wailed a deep, long, baleful cry.

104

Scarface switched off his flashlight, so the boys could not see what was happening, but they could easily hear footsteps as the men started running, but they were running directly at the boys. At the very same moment, the boys rushed forward, colliding with Scarface and Slouch Hat in the dark. Everyone went down. A few punches were thrown in the blackness, although none took effect. Tweed reached for Doc's arm and started to pull him away from the melee, when Scarface's flashlight lighted up the passage in a blinding white light. A shocked Tweed discovered that he was not holding hands with Doc, but with Slouch Hat. The big man grabbed him back. Scarface grappled with Doc, quickly pinned his arms to the ground, although the boy was able to land a solid right to the man's jaw during the scuffle and kicked him good in the stomach.

"We've finally got these meddling kids this time," said Slouch Hat to his companion. "Douse the light again before that pirate's ghost or whatever it is grabs us."

The men pulled out ropes they had tucked in their back pockets and tied the boy's wrists tightly, leaving a long leash to hold onto them.

The light went out, and the men held the boys on the ground, unable to move. To the boys, it seemed like an hour had passed, as the four of them waited in the murky blackness. Clearly the men weren't sure if they should expect an attack from their spectral visitor. Despite their hearing an occasional stone drop to the floor now and then from different directions, nothing else indicated if the smuggler's ghost, or something else, haunted the cave.

"Okay," said Slouch Hat. "There's nothing out there. Let's get our little buddies back to the main chamber. There's been too much strange stuff in this cave for my liking, but nothing's ever bothered us in the main chamber. It seems to like the back of the cave where it is dark and wet."

"I think we should just get out of this boogeyman's cave as fast as we can and let the other guys come for the stuff," said Scarface. "I don't like any part of this evil spirit, and now we know those Indians were right about this place."

"What? And goof up the whole gig? The boat'll be here in a little over an hour. Then we're out of this state for good. All we have to do is keep these pesky kids tied up and keep our eyes open. If Pig's-Eye's ghost shows actually, we'll take off and leave the kids for his lunch."

The men heaved the boys to their feet and shoved them in the direction of the main chamber. Stumbling and struggling, the boys were forced to walk ahead of the men.

"You creeps'll never get away with this," said Doc, as he continued to struggle against the ropes. "Our families and the police know we're here. And if I get these confounded ropes off, my fists won't be done with you."

"Why you little punk . . ." Scarface said. "I'll—"

"Lay off the kid . . . least for now," said a somewhat angry Slouch Hat. "Both these brats'll be fish food in a few hours anyway. Just watch where you're walking here in the dark. We are almost back to the chamber. There, see the lights from the lanterns up ahead? Another couple hours, this caper'll be finished, and we'll be ready for another strike somewhere else with lots of dough in our pockets."

Following a bit of physical resistance from Doc, who nearly pulled away from his captor, the men and their prisoners entered the lighted chamber. Without saying a word, they took some more rope from a trunk full of tools and tied the two boys back to back against one of the bicycle racks. They struggled with their bonds but were unable to free themselves.

Slouch Hat roared with hoarse laughter as he watched them. "Better get comfortable, boys," he said. "You're going to be here for the rest of your lives. You might say that we're nice guys to show you your tombs while you're still alive. Now that's a luxury most people don't get."

He doubled over with laughter, panting as if he would lose his breath. Scarface also chuckled, the ghost in the tunnel only a memory. Then Slouch Hat gave both boys a stern look and addressed them rudely, "You little rats come clean with us now. How'd you get wise to us? Why have you been following us?"

At first the boys said nothing, but when Slouch Hat threatened to backhand Doc across the face, the boy said, "We were just poking around, looking for the cave. We didn't even know you guys were here. Then we saw your head stick up, and we wanted to know what was going on."

Tweed added, "We saw those kids bringing those stolen bikes to you from the balloon. We figured you guys had a pretty good racket going, and that takes a lot of brains. We talked it over and agreed that we could steal you a couple racing bikes worth a couple grand. We still could if you let us go."

"Don't trust those punks," interjected Scarface. "They've been doing too much snooping around to be anything but dime-droppers."

Tweed yelled at him, "Well, how in heaven's name do you know you can trust the other kids that work for you?"

"We have five kids stealing bikes for us in St. Paul. Believe me, they can all be trusted. Let' say—"

"Don't tell 'em anything, you fool," shouted a perturbed Scarface.

"What's the difference," snapped Slouch Hat. "They're never going to be able to tell anybody."

"That's right," Tweed said. "If we're going to die, why not tell us everything?"

"Ya wanna know the setup, do you? Fine. I'll let you in on a little secret. You wanted it, you'll get it. You can have the whole story, and when I am finished, you'll be meat for Pig's-Eye's ghost."

"I dunno if you should blab anything to these kids," cautioned Scarface, who kept one eye glued towards the back of the cave where they had heard the warning from beyond. "There are spooks in this cave, and it's like every rock has ears. I say let's just vamoose and wait outside in the brush for the boat."

Tweed watched Slouch Hat, knowing he wanted to brag about his victory. He was ready to spill the beans on the whole set-up, and Tweed thought maybe keeping him talking would keep them alive a little longer. Slouch Hat, proud as a peacock, directed an uneasy glance at the blackness of the "ghost" passage, sat down somewhat comfortably on a flat surfaced rock and began his story:

"You dumb kids stumbled upon the biggest bicycle smuggling ring in the country, and it would have been better for you if you hadn't. We work one city at a time, and we select only the high-dollar bikes—the best in customs, mountains, and racers. Of course, we need to employ some kids who don't ask many questions and can steal the bikes. We only use teens who'll work for nothing and that means we have to get something on them. In your town, we picked up five kids—runaways—and told them we were police detectives. They were scared, plenty scared. And they believed every word we said. We told 'em some other kids had been stealing the nice bikes, but we knew who they were and where the stolen bikes were. All we wanted was to get those bikes back to their owners. The dumb kids believed us. We'd point out the bikes and tell them to bring them to the 'police' cave, or we'd send them to juvenile detention. They've done a nice job, picked up 284 top-of-the-line bikes, which, of course, weren't stolen until our kids took them. Each one will bring a pretty penny.

"At midnight tonight, and that's only an hour away, the rest of our gang'll arrive by boat on the Mississippi. When they get close, the captain will flash his light a couple times, and we'll be in the entrance flashing our light back at him. Once they've got our exact position in the dark, they'll glide her up to the bank, and a ramp'll be extended from the boat to shore. Then we load all the bikes and head down river to another port where we sell the bikes for big bucks. A few of 'em we have to repaint or make a few adjustments on before we sell but they'll all find happy homes, and we'll never come back to your town again."

"Happy home nothing," snapped an angry Doc. "What about the unhappy homes you create by your lowdown thievery? And getting poor, homeless kids to do your dirty work. You're the slimiest scum on earth, and you'll pay for your treachery!"

"Stop it!" Slouch Hat laughed. "You're breaking my heart."

"And what about us?" inquired Tweed. "I suppose you crooks plan to take us with you."

"Oh, no, we're not that cruel. We certainly wouldn't want to harm you boys. No, we've got better plans for you. Much better!"

Scarface stepped forward and said to his partner in crime: "I'm going to go wait by the entrance for the boys to get here with the boat. I can't bear to watch these kids get swallowed up by that smuggler's ghost. Have fun, kids, and tell old Pierre thanks for allowing us to share his cave with him." He disappeared down the entrance passage, laughing and pointing. Slouch Hat watched him go.

"You know, you pesky kids kept us on our toes," snarled Slouch Hat. "I wish I could let you go, but we all know better than that. When we leave, we'll be sealing up the entrance. You'll be locked in here with Parrant's ghost. Don't holler too loud, and we might leave the light on for you."

"Then you don't plan to harm us?" speculated Tweed.

The man laughed. "Us? Why, no! We won't have to. By the time someone finds their way into this cave, all they'll find will be two rotted skeletons. There really is no escape, you know!"

Chapter Ten

light in the night

Doc gave Tweed a horrified glance and again confronted Slouch Hat. "You're not so tough, you know, picking on kids. I saw that guy at the fair toss you guys around like two pieces of cardboard."

"That punk will get his," snarled Slouch Hat, while resting his head on the cavern wall.

No one said a word over the next ten minutes as the boys watched their captor's head droop and eyes open and close. Finally, his eyes stayed shut, and both boys were convinced they could hear him snoring. One of the lanterns flickered but did not go out as Tweed gently nudged his companion and lowered his chin to get Doc's attention. Doc's eyes followed those of Tweed to a sharp rock jutting out of the ground only inches away from them.

"If we can maneuver a couple inches to that rock," whispered Tweed, "we can cut the ropes off our wrists. We'll have to work together see-saw fashion. If we can get me loose, I'll untie you and maybe we can scram while that thug's sawing logs."

"But where can we go even if we do get loose?" asked Doc. "That other big bruiser's blocking the entrance, and there's no other way out. We're still trapped."

"I have an idea. For now, let's keep quiet and not wake him up. Let's concentrate on getting these ropes off."

Both boys stretched and slid sideways from a sitting position. With their legs bound tightly, every inch was crucial in securing their possible freedom. Their slight movement cast waltzing shadows upon the cavern wall, and each kept an eye on their dozing captor in fear he would awaken. An inch . . . two . . . another.

With the rock between them, they began sliding the rope binding Tweed's wrists back and forth over the jagged edge at sharp angles. The knife-like surface snagged and chaffed their skin, and they could not seem to work the knots of their bonds loose. Their muscles throbbed with the effort of rubbing their arms back and forth, trying to saw through the ropes that held them fast.

Tweed thought he felt a little give in the rough cords, the slightest bit of slack, and that was the only reason they were able to continue their seemingly hopeless attempt at freedom. As they rubbed the rope along the edges of the rock, Tweed's fingers picked awkwardly at the knots. Finally, Tweed felt the rope binding his wrists start to fray and unravel. His fingers started picking at the strands, and all at once they seemed to come apart, untwisting with the simplest actions of plucking and pulling. He felt the bonds pull apart, and the ropes loosened, loops rolling from his wrists. He rotated his wrists, gaining inches. Suddenly he was free.

With an eye on the sleeping Slouch Hat, Tweed ripped at the rope holding his ankles. When he felt it give, he made an effort to get on his knees and free Doc. The pain in his arms and legs, however, nearly caused him to groan out loud, and he fell back to a sitting position and rubbed his ankles to get the blood circulating again. He continued his massaging for three or four minutes before he arose ever so carefully. This time the pain was much less severe, and he quickly but quietly untied the ropes holding Doc.

Having witnessed the pain Tweed had suffered in his first attempt to kneel, Doc stayed put for several minutes and extended his arms and legs in a comical but important stretching ritual. He, too, glared at his sleeping captor as he got up slowly with help from Tweed.

"Now one of us has to tiptoe behind Slouch Hat and snatch a couple of those lanterns without waking him," whispered Tweed, taking a step forward. He felt Doc's hand on his arm.

"I'll get them. Stay here," said Doc so low that Tweed only received the message by reading his friend's lips.

Before Tweed could object, Doc had crept behind the sleeping smuggler and secured two lanterns. Just as he started back, he froze as Slouch Hat mumbled something unintelligible in his sleep and shifted his position. Doc froze, his eyes wide, but soon the steady pattern of Slouch Hat's breathing returned. Doc tiptoed the ten feet back to Tweed, and the two boys, each with a lantern, moved unseen into the deep recesses of the catacomb.

As they moved worm-like through the passage, Tweed placed a hand on his friend's shoulder and said softly, "You know what I'm thinking, don't you . . . ?"

"I think so," replied Doc, tripping on a stone and nearly falling. "The ghost, right? The ghost of Pig's-Eye Parrant?"

"Exactly! You recognized that voice, didn't you?"

"Of course! I knew it didn't come from a ghost, although I bet there are a few in here. It was Andy's voice we heard. I'd know it anywhere. He must have known we were in trouble but couldn't find the entrance to the cave. And I have a feeling he is still out there."

"Now think! Andy is out there and knows we are in a big jam. He faked the voice of Pig's-Eye to make Scarface and Slouch Hat think there really is a ghost in here. They were plenty scared too. We only heard the voice in one area of the cave, and it seemed to come from above. Do you remember that spot?"

"Of course, I do! Just this side of that dangerous pit, like out of that little side shaft I crawled in and met a dead-end. That's it, Tweed. The voice came out of that shaft, and I remember there was a very, very faint light in the ceiling, or at least it seemed so. Sure, that's it! Andy was, and maybe still is, above that shaft. He found a hole in the ground probably not bigger than an acorn and yelled into it. That means if we're going to try and contact him, we have to go back into that little tunnel and yell up to him."

"But it'll be dangerous. Slouch Hat is bound to hear us yelling. Then he'll get Scarface and catch us all over again."

"So what do we do?"

"We're not going to approach it like that. What I'm thinking is a real long shot. It probably won't work, but it may be our only chance of warning Andy about the boat coming in and those creeps from getting away clean with all those bikes, not to mention getting us out of here alive."

"Okay, but . . . what do we do? Somehow I get the feeling this is going to involve me and not you. But let's get cooking. Old Slouch Hat's probably awake by now, and the two of them already coming for us. When they catch us this time, it'll be much worse for us."

"I know. I'm scared too. The point is that you know Morse Code and I don't. I remember you telling me you learned it in a special class in Chicago last year. Hope that was for real."

"I took the class, but I . . ."

"You didn't exactly get an 'A.' I know. But you know how to send a message, and you can send all those dots and dashes with your hand over your lantern in that shaft. Just aim it towards that hole you think is above there. If Andy is up there and peering into that hole, he'll should be able to make out those lights flickering on and off through the darkness. He's a whiz at lots of codes, including Morse. Heck, I saw you guys last summer sending signals back and forth. You told me Andy was a radio operator in the navy and learned the code systems there. I know for a fact that the navy uses light signals. He's got to know them."

The duo continued on through the passage, their footsteps echoing through the subterranean tunnel, despite their stepping lightly. Tweed pointed ahead to the shaft, and Doc ran ahead with his lantern, crawled within it, holding his lantern ahead of him and stopped directly under what he perceived to be a tiny air hole in the cavern roof. Tweed stuck his head into the shaft and asked, "Do you know what you're doing?"

"I think so. I even remember part of the manual word for word." As he positioned himself and got ready, he recited what to do to steady his hands: "If the duration of a dot is taken to be one unit, then that of a dash is three units. The space between the components of one character is one unit, between characters is three units and between words . . . seven units. I sure hope that's right."

"Just get to it with as few words as possible. We are running out of time."

Doc was silent as he worked the shutter on the lantern. Tweed watched the strange flashing dots and dashes lighting up the tiny chamber with the low, vaulted ceiling. The kaleidoscopic display bouncing off the walls like bolts of lightning reminded him of two summers past when he and Doc helped capture a criminal disguised as a clown at an Independence Day fireworks celebration at Lake Nokomis.

He was brought back to the present by Doc backing out of the shaft, covered with dirt. Tweed looked at him and said, "You look like a miner, Doc!"

"I sent the message twice," Doc said. "Prisoners . . . Call police . . . Boat on river at midnight to pick up stolen goods . . . Lights to flash from boat and cave."

Tweed helped his friend to his feet. "Do you think Andy was still there and got your message?"

"I don't know. I hope so."

Suddenly both boys turned in fear as a terrifying, distant voice rumbled from deep within the shaft Doc had just exited: "This is the Ghost of Pig's-Eye Parrant. Beware!"

Then all was silent.

"Andy!" cried both boys in unison in harsh whispers.

"He's still out there and got the message," exclaimed Doc.

"But let's hope our two smuggler friends heard it too and are afraid to come back here. Come on. Let's move a little deeper into the cave. At least it is nice to know that Pig's-Eye is on our side."

They moved a little deeper into Fountain Cave and sat down on the ground about fifty feet from the yawning chasm. Even though they could walk around it, they feared the pit and the unknown horrors that lurked within it. Doc walked carefully to the edge of the precipice, holding his lantern above his head, and dropped a tiny stone into his depths. He wasn't certain but he thought he had heard it hit water. It took a long second or two to reach it, though.

"I think there's water down there," he told a more cautious Tweed. "You're the walking encyclopedia. I'm wondering if it would be safe to hide down there. The crooks might not follow us down there."

"Most caves have several galleries on different levels and have passed through several phases," offered Tweed. "Only a few are without a cave stream. When caves with a stream come into contact with limestone, they sink and create cave galleries. Some caves have vertical pit-like channels like that one that are very deep. There's no way we're risking our lives by climbing down there. It must be close to midnight now and that phantom boat'll be arriving before we know it. We'll wait here and try to buy some time for Andy to do his work."

The boys extinguished their lanterns and crouched on the damp floor, fearing that at any minute their two adversaries would recapture them. All was silent for nearly ten minutes when the faint glow of a lantern ricocheted off the cavern walls where the passageway flexed its elbow in a forty-five-degree turn.

"Come on," whispered Tweed. "We have to get deeper into the cave. Keep that lantern out."

"But we may flop into that pit in front of us in the blackness," replied Doc, cautiously groping his way through the passage.

"The pit should be just a few feet in front of us. Hold my hand. I'll inch forward. I should be able to feel the drop without falling in."

"Okay, you brats," boomed a deep gruff voice from behind them. "We know you're back here. This time it's curtains for you. Ghost or no ghost, we're coming for you."

Dangling a leg over the edge of the abyss, Tweed pulled back with help from Doc. "Okay," he mumbled, speaking low enough to prevent an echo. "We know the parameters of the pit. Walk slowly to your left until you touch the wall. Then slide along it until you're sure you've passed the pit."

Both boys edged their way past the pit as the footfalls of their pursuers reverberated not too far behind them. Tweed told Doc to quickly light his lantern and stand directly behind the pit. His plan was obvious to the boy from Illinois. In seconds he had the light glowing. Doc waved his lantern back and forth in front of his face and both boys taunted the smugglers by calling them names and laughing at them.

Scarface and Slouch Hat vented their anger and lunged forward at their quarry, growling like two hungry lions. At that same moment, Doc extinguished his lantern and yelled, "Let's outrun these bums."

"They're right in front of us," bellowed one of the smugglers with his arms extended.

Doc roared back, "You couldn't catch a rabbit if it was tied to your thumb."

"I'll get—" Slouch Hat never finished his threat. Then the boys heard two heavy wet thuds.

"It worked! It worked!" yelled a jubilant Doc. "They took the bait and fell in." Relighting his lantern, he peered over the edge and thought he saw two tragic figures squirming like worms perhaps thirty feet below, moaning and groaning. "You guys comfortable down there?"

A series of incoherent threats seemed to shoot up from the depths of the pit. Tweed winked at Doc and giggled, "At least they're in one piece. Let's get out of here and warn Andy."

Two boys never ran through a St. Paul cave as fast as Tweed and Doc did at that moment. Of course, they circumvented the pit before throwing their gears in motion, and as they rounded the turn in the passageway, they resembled front-runners in an Olympic marathon with the last 100 yards in sight. Losing not a minute, they rushed through the chamber of stolen bicycles, into the passage leading to the entrance, and pushed open the secret doorway to the night sky.

Neither boy had expected to see such a welcoming committee: Andy and his friend Wally, Sergeant Berven, several St. Paul police officers, and even a newspaper reporter who had responded to a lucky tip. Andy hugged both boys as tears cascaded down his cheeks. Tweed and Doc gasped at the same time, each trying to relate his own version of the stolen bikes caper and the mysterious boat about to arrive to pick them up.

"It's about ten minutes to twelve," announced Sergeant Berven in a voice of authority. "Everybody take cover. That boat'll be coming along any minute. I want those guys, too."

Men and boys alike concealed themselves in the tall grass and behind rocks along the rugged cliff face. Sergeant Berven checked with an officer named Ledford to make sure he had his light in hand, and a call was put in for the river cops to bring up a boat.

Nothing happened for fifteen minutes. Then the low hum of an engine moving down river began to grow lower. A moment later, the beam of light illuminated the center of the river. The big moment had come!

A signal light flashed twice on the riverbank, somewhat off target and a hundred feet to their right. Officer Ledford quickly answered with two flashing beams. Again, the light from the boat flashed their way, this time much closer to where the party on shore lay in wait. After several exchanges of lights, the boat was steered in close to the bank, and a voice cried out, "Pierce, is that you?"

"Come on in," yelled one of the officers. "Got a great load for you this time."

The boat came as close to shore as was safe, and someone aboard laid down a long metal ramp that reached the shore. Three burly men tramped down the ramp, followed by their captain, a lean but wiry chap with a handlebar moustache and long sideburns. It was he that Sergeant Berven grabbed from behind and proclaimed, "Okay, Elvis, you and your crew are under arrest."

Although the other three rascals put up quite a fight, they were no match for the well-trained police officers, who had the whole gang handcuffed in a matter of minutes. As the captain pleaded his innocence, a few of the officers boarded the boat in search of other lawbreakers and any additional contraband.

The boat consisted of two levels, the upper forming a sort of balcony looking down on the main, lower level. There were large windows looking out over the river. The floating pirate ship was fairly well lit by the usual garish neon of similar crafts.

"Anybody here want to buy a bike?" jested Sergeant Berven, but none of the prisoners mumbled a word.

The river cops boat arrived, and squad cars filled the parking lot above. The boat crew, handcuffed and subdued, were led away from the cave. Other police checked out the stolen bicycles in the cave, the sergeant admitted he was shocked that such a large operation had been thriving right under his nose. He said, "These guys are going away for a long, long time."

Turning to Tweed and Doc, he said: "You boys are genuine heroes. If it hadn't been for you two, these creeps may have gotten away with this caper. On the other hand, you could have been killed. Since you weren't, I'm going to call you into police headquarters for a special recognition ceremony. And there must be rewards out on some of these guys. You kids could get a bundle for this. How does that sound?"

"If it is all the same to you," replied a cheerful Tweed, "we'd like to give the reward money to those poor kids forced to steal the bikes. I'll bet you can get their names out of Slouch Hat and Scarface. Doc and I think they're just nice kids badly in need of a break."

During the excitement, both boys had completely forgotten about Slouch Hat and Scarface imprisoned in the cavern pit. They quickly told the police about the two smugglers floundering in their underground prison.

Twenty minutes later, officers brought the badly bruised pair out of the cave in handcuffs. "Outsmarted by a couple kids," muttered one of them. "I can't believe this."

"You can believe one thing—you won't see another bicycle until the 2020 models come out," quipped Sergeant Berven. "Officer Ledford, read them their rights, please."

After thanking the boys for their detective work and courage, the police marched their prisoners away.

Andy led Doc and Tweed to the now well-worn path leading to the parking lot. "I'm really proud of you boys, but you sure gave Elizabeth, Grandfather West, and me a huge scare," said Andy. "You could have been killed."

The boys hung their heads.

Suddenly Andy's sternness evaporated. He ruffled their hair and said, "Let's go home for a late supper."

They clambered up to the parking lot on Shepard Road. Andy said, "We had to call your folks, Doc. You know that."

"I guess. They'll never let me come back, will they?"

Andy laughed. "Actually, I talked with your dad after we found you. He's relieved you're okay. We talked about working out something so you can come back for a brief visit the weekend after Labor Day for the Defeat of Jesse James Celebration in Northfield. I go every year, and it's lots of fun. There's a mock robbery, horses, lots of gunfights, and all of it true history."

"Really? You think he'd let me come?"

"You'll have to swear not to get into trouble, of course, but there aren't any caves down there."

"We can't possibly get into any trouble there, Andy," ventured Tweed, "unless Doc eats too many foot-long hotdogs and has to go to the hospital. What say, Doc, no trouble?"

The other boy only winked as the four started for Andy's truck. Turning their backs on Fountain Cave, they had taken but a step or two when they heard a high-pitched howling and what sounded like actual syllables. They quickened their pace.

"Maybe the ghost of Pig's-Eye Parrant really does haunt that cave," said Andy. "That sure sounded real. But, of course, we know that there's no such thing as ghosts, don't we boys?"

"Of course, we do," replied Doc. "But just in case there are, let's get out of here."

Tweed paused at the edge of the embankment, his eyes fixed on the cave entrance a minute or two, as the others started across the parking lot to the truck. "Of course," he said under his breath. "Of course!"

THE END